THE JUNIOR NOVELIZATION

Published in the United States by Random House Children's Books, a division of
Random House, Inc., 1745 Broadway, New York, NY 10019, and in Canada by Random
House of Canada Limited, Toronto, in conjunction with Disney Enterprises, Inc. Random
House and the colophon are registered trademarks of Random House, Inc.

ISBN: 978-0-7364-2814-9

www. randomhouse.com/kids

Printed in the United States of America
10 9 8 7 6 5 4 3 2 1

THE JUNIOR NOVELIZATION

Adapted by Irene Trimble

Random House New York

"This is Agent Leland Turbo," the British spy car whispered hurriedly. "I have a flash transmission for Agent Finn McMissile." Turbo was looking directly into the camera of his audiovisual transmitter, trying to reach headquarters. The agent quickly spun and checked to see if his enemies were approaching. Safe so far. "You won't believe what I've found out here. This is bigger than anything we've ever seen. And no one knows it exists."

The audio static was making Turbo's message nearly indecipherable, but some of his words were crystal clear: "Finn, I need backup!" The transmission flickered. Then Turbo added, "Transmitting my grids now. Good luck."

Hours later, in the pitch-dark night, a feisty little boat fearlessly made its way through the rough seas of the North Pacific. It stayed on course as its bow alternately rose and slammed down into the oncoming swells.

On board, Agent Finn McMissile steeled himself as the boat approached the coordinates designated on his dashboard. As one of Britain's best spies, Finn had serious business to address tonight—clandestine business.

"All right, we're here—right where you paid me to bring you," Finn's scrappy ride told him as they rocked from side to side. "The question is: Why?"

"To find a car," Finn answered elusively.

The tiny boat glanced back at his rider. "I hate to break it to you, but there ain't nobody out here."

Finn braced his tires. The little boat was wrong about that. The agency had tracked Finn's fellow agent Turbo to these very coordinates. Turbo was somewhere out here, and he was in trouble. Turbo also had information—important, top-secret information.

Suddenly, the bright light of a massive combat ship targeted the little boat. Finn took this as a signal that they were close to his enemy. No one else around here would have high security. He quickly backed into the shadows.

The combat ship suddenly swung a laser beam directly at the boat and ordered, "Turn around and go back where you came from."

"Sorry, buddy," the boat said to Finn. "Guess this is as far as we go."

But no one answered. Finn McMissile was gone.

As the combat ship navigated the turbulent waters, Finn hung off the large vessel's side, unseen. A sudden discharge of orange flame briefly illuminated the darkness. In the flash, Finn could see that the ship was pulling alongside a huge oil derrick.

He quickly released a high-tech tether that held him to the side of the ship, and drove up to one of the higher platforms. The deck below him was crawling with cheap cars—likely inexpensive labor for whoever was running this place. Gremlins and Pacers unloaded crate after crate from a large cargo boat.

Then Finn heard the unmistakable sound of German engineering. A boxlike blue-green car, wearing a monocle, rolled onto the deck and began shouting orders.

"Too many cars here! Out of the way!"

Finn instantly recognized the car: Professor Z. He was a gifted German scientist whose specialty was designing weapons. He was also at the top of Britain's Most Wanted list. Professor Z was willing to do any work—terrible and destructive work—for anyone willing to pay the right price.

"Here it is, Professor," a Pacer said as he hovered next to a crate. "You wanted to see this before we loaded it?" Not even Finn recognized the American agent Rod Redline, working undercover as a Pacer.

"Ah, yes," Professor Z answered. "Show me, please. Very carefully."

Finn silently fired off a grappling hook and slid to the other side of the oil derrick. He watched as a forklift lowered and opened the mysterious crate. Inside was a TV camera packed as carefully as a brand-new windshield. The letters WGP stood out on its side.

Professor Z was most pleased. "Good, good," he said with a thick German accent. "This is valuable equipment. Make sure it is properly secured for the voyage."

Gremlins and Pacers surrounded the crate and began closing it up. Apparently, they were sending it away with the cargo boat. Finn made a note to himself to find out where that cargo boat was headed.

As the secret agent snapped photos, something else caught his attention. A crane lowered another large crate to the deck for Professor Z's inspection.

"Hey, Professor Z!" a Gremlin, aptly named Grem, shouted. "This is one of those British spies we told you about."

Professor Z knew exactly who it was: "Agent Leland Turbo."

Finn got ready to come out of hiding and fight.

Finn McMissile's eyes widened when he finally saw Turbo: the agent was already crushed and cubed.

A blast of flame from the oil derrick suddenly cast Finn's shadow onto Professor Z. The Professor made eye contact with his nemesis.

"It's Finn McMissile!" Professor Z shouted to his thugs, ordering them to chase down the spy.

Gremlins, Pacers, and other shoddy cars swarmed onto the catwalk closest to Finn. But Finn was faster and more agile. He shot out his cables, latching on to the crane standing tall above the deck. Nimbly, he swung out and drove straight up the crane's arm, away from the chase. The agent used every trick he could think of to escape. First he released some oil, causing his pursuers to spin out behind him; then he knocked over a stack of oil drums, blocking their path. But when Finn reached the helipad on the top deck of the oil derrick, there was nowhere left to go. The enemy cars surrounded him, their tinny engines whining like a swarm of mosquitoes.

Finn slammed into reverse . . . and flung himself off the side of the oil derrick. He hit the water hundreds of feet below.

Gremlins and Pacers raced to stare down into the turbulent ocean. In a burst of splashing water, Finn surfaced and transformed into a sleek hydrofoil. He sped away from the oil derrick.

"He's getting away!" Acer the Pacer shouted.

"Not for long," a combat ship replied as he released two missiles. The cars on the derrick watched as the missiles exploded. Finn's motionless silhouette drifted under the surface of the ocean. Shortly afterward, all four of his tires floated to the surface. Professor Z smiled and called off the chase. It had been a wonderful night. Both Finn McMissile and Leland Turbo had been eliminated.

"Now no one can stop us," Professor Z told his grinning crew.

But he was wrong: Finn McMissile had transformed into submarine mode and purposely released his tires. As his enemies on the oil derrick turned away, Finn was speeding underwater to return to agency headquarters.

At the crack of dawn on the following day, halfway around the world, a rusty, dented tow truck named Mater had his eyes fixed on Route 66, smack in the middle of the U.S.A. Lightning McQueen was returning to Radiator Springs fresh from winning the Hudson Hornet Memorial Piston Cup race. Mater couldn't wait to see him.

Things had improved mightily since racing champion Lightning McQueen had made Radiator Springs his permanent home. Tourists visited regularly, and the whole dusty town had taken on a shine like a new coat of chrome. And no one enjoyed the reflected glory of Lightning McQueen's success more than his buddy Mater.

"I'm gonna stay right here in this spot until my best friend, Lightning McQueen, comes home," Mater said, bleary-eyed and exhausted.

Lightning's girlfriend, Sally, was worried. She and Mater were the only two cars in town who were awake.

"Mater," Sally said with a weary sigh, "you've been sitting here for seven days."

"That's 'cause I got a special surprise for him, Miss Sally," Mater replied. "To celebrate his fourth Piston Cup win. And I want to show it to him first thing."

"Okay," Sally said, driving off. "At least move around a little. Your gaskets are gonna dry up. You're gonna leak oil."

"I never leak oil!" Mater called after her.

But Mater had a bigger problem: he simply could not stay awake any longer.

Later that day, as Mater snored and snored, Lightning McQueen finally arrived home. All of Lightning's friends were gathered around, eager to see him. Sally nuzzled next to him. And, of course, there was Ramone, the owner of the body shop, and Flo, his wife, who ran the newly refurbished Wheel Well restaurant. Sarge and Fillmore were there, too. Sarge owned the surplus supplies store right next to Fillmore's, where the green-and-white van made and sold his own organic fuel. Lizzie, the old black car who owned the curio shop, was settled right next to Red, the fire truck.

Poor Mater had waited the longest for Lightning

to return, and now he was missing the homecoming!

"He looks so peaceful," Lightning said. "I don't want to wake him up."

"Okay, move aside!" It was Mack, the big rig who drove Lightning to and from his races. "I've always wanted to do this."

The big rig blasted his horn, startling Mater so wide awake that the poor tow truck raced around town backward at top speed—he couldn't stop!

Finally, Mater drove right over a cliff! "I'm okay!" he shouted as all his friends raced to his rescue. He had already tossed his hook over a ledge and was climbing back into view.

"Mater?" Lightning shouted, worried about his pal.

"I'm all right," Mater said.

But Lightning was concerned. "Wow, you just got yourself a nasty dent there, buddy."

"That might be my best dent yet!" Mater said proudly. He grinned at Lightning. Mater's dents were a sign of friendship and of his many adventures with Lightning. He had gotten dents while tractor-tipping with Lightning, while pulling the race car out of ditches, and even while showing off his backward driving. He'd kept every dent he'd ever gotten as a way to remember good times with his best friend.

"Mater, it's so good to see you!" Lightning exclaimed as soon as he knew Mater was okay.

"You, too, buddy!" Mater shouted. "Oh! I got something to show you! You're gonna love it."

"Actually," Lightning said quietly, "I've got something to show you first."

Lightning and Mater drove to Doc Hudson's former garage. The town had converted it into a racing museum in Doc's honor. Lightning placed his trophy—the first-ever Hudson Hornet Memorial Piston Cup—in the case alongside Doc's and his own Piston Cups.

"I know Doc said these things were just old cups . . . but to have someone else win it just didn't feel right, you know?" Lightning said quietly.

Mater nodded. "Doc would've been mighty proud of you," he said. "That's for sure."

The private moment ended as the two friends took off to join the rest of the Radiator Springs citizens.

"Boy, I'll tell you what, pal," Lightning said to Mater as they drove along together. "It's been a long day. All I want to do is—"

"Stay up all night and party?" Mater asked excitedly as they moved toward his salvage yard.

"No. . . ." Lightning hesitated.

Mater grinned. "Go tractor-tipping, then stay up all night long?"

"No, Mater. I want to go out for a quiet dinner," Lightning said.

"That sounds like fun, too!" Mater agreed. "Exactly what I was thinking!"

Lightning paused. "I meant with Sally, Mater," he managed to say.

"That's a great idea!" Mater's grin got even wider. "You, me, and Miss Sally going out for supper! Where we gonna eat? Hey, I know—how about that new restaurant at the water park down on the interstate—Kersploosh Mountain?"

Lightning was hoping he wouldn't hurt Mater's feelings, but he really wanted to spend special time alone with Sally. "I was kind of thinking it would be a romantic dinner."

"Well, dadgum. You can't get more romantic than Kersploosh Mountain. I hear tell they got slides where two cars can ride down together!" Mater said as they reached the salvage yard.

And with that, Mater got ready to connect the battery to his big surprise. It was a "Welcome Home" display he had made especially for Lightning. He was so excited that he could hardly contain himself.

"Mater," Lightning blurted out. "I meant it would be just me and Sally."

Mater stopped short. His smile dropped just a bit. Trying to hide his disappointment—and his light-up sign—he looked down at his tires.

"Oh."

"It's just for tonight," Lightning said gently.

"Uh, okay," Mater said, glancing at his big sign in disappointment. "Yeah."

"Thanks for understanding." Lightning revved his engine. "I'm going to go tell Sally."

"Right now?" Mater could hardly keep his lower lip from quivering.

"Yeah. Oh, wait! You wanted to show me something."

"Oh, no. It was nothing. It can wait." Mater faked a grin for his buddy. "You go on and have fun!"

Lightning sped away.

Alone now, Mater let out a big sigh. He had worked for days to create Lightning's surprise. He couldn't help himself. He turned, attached some jumper cables to a battery, and watched his contraption come to life.

A car horn played a celebratory song as an elaborate sign rose from behind a pile of tires. The sign read WELCOME HOME, BEST FRIEND!

As a final touch, two panels dropped and revealed two oilcans—one labeled with Lightning's name and the other with Mater's name. Mater's disappointment disappeared in a flash. Those old oilcans gave him an idea!

Later in the evening, Lightning and Sally left the glow of Radiator Springs' soft neon lights and drove up the moonlit mountain to the Wheel Well Motel's newly decorated restaurant.

They had just settled down and were enjoying the view from their table when their waiter appeared. Lightning looked up and did a double take. It was Mater. He was dressed in a waiter's uniform!

"Good evening," Mater announced carefully. (He had received some quick training to ensure that he served Lightning and Sally their dinner just right.) "My name is Mater. I'll be your waiter this evening." Then he chuckled. "Mater the waiter. That's pretty funny right there."

"Mater, do you work here?" Lightning asked.

"Yeah," Mater answered, grinning widely at the

couple. "What'd you think? I was pretending to be your waiter just to hang out with you?"

Lightning and Sally exchanged a look. They knew Mater just wanted to be near his best friend.

"Uh, this wasn't my idea," Lightning whispered to Sally.

But Sally just smiled. She knew how much Lightning meant to Mater. She decided to play along. "Okay, then, what are the specials tonight, Mater the waiter?"

Mater looked at Sally blankly. "The specials? Oh. Well, our transmission consommé is sublime."

Sally was stunned—and delighted—by Mater's presentation. Lightning was impressed.

"Ooh, I think I saw Miss Sally's eyes light up there," Lightning commented. "What else you got?"

Mater grinned. "There's coolant gas-pacho. That's served cold. And it's drizzled with power-steering fluid." Mater went on and on until he couldn't think of any other dishes. "I'll let you two lovebirds mull that over while I get your drinks."

Lightning grinned. He had to hand it to Mater: the tow truck had done well.

"I'll have my usual," he told Mater.

"That sounds good. I'll have his usual, too," Sally said. She liked seeing Lightning and Mater together. Their friendship was important to both of them.

Mater blinked. Clearly, he would have to figure out what that "usual" was! He turned and drove away to find out.

"I really missed that guy," Lightning said to Sally. "Never a dull moment."

4

Inside the restaurant, Fillmore and Sarge were watching television as Guido served the cars some fuel and oil.

"Guido," Mater said in a hushed voice, "what's Lightning's usual?"

Guido replied—in Italian—that he had no idea.

"Perfect!" Mater agreed. "Give me two of them!"

As Mater waited for Guido to pour some oil into two glasses, his attention strayed to the television. *The Mel Dorado Show* was on. Mel's guest tonight was legendary oil baron Sir Miles Axlerod.

"He shocked the world when he sold his oil fortune, converted himself from a gas guzzler into an electric car, and devoted his life to finding a renewable, clean-burning fuel!" Mel announced over the TV.

"Once 'big oil,' always 'big oil,' man," Fillmore commented. He preferred his own organic blend.

"And to show the world what his new superfuel, Allinol, can do," Mel told his viewing audience, "he's created a racing competition like no other, inviting the greatest champions from around the globe to battle in the first-ever World Grand Prix!"

Axlerod nodded modestly.

"Why Allinol? Why now?" Mel asked.

"Have you filled up your tank recently? It costs a fortune," Sir Miles replied. "Pollution is getting worse. The world is sick of 'big oil.'" Impassioned, Axlerod went on, "Alternative fuel is the future! And Allinol is the cleanest, safest, cheapest alternative fuel ever made." Mel nodded approvingly as Axlerod continued. "Trust me, Mel. After seeing Allinol in action at the World Grand Prix, nobody will ever go back to gasoline again."

Mel asked Miles why Lightning McQueen hadn't been invited to be in the race.

"We did ask," Axlerod replied. "But apparently he's taking some time off to rest."

At that moment, the Italian racing legend

Francesco Bernoulli jumped into the conversation.

"Lightning McQueen would not have a chance against Francesco!" Francesco boasted.

Mater's jaw dropped. He could not believe that this Italian racer was insulting Lightning on TV! Mater put down his tray and headed for the phone.

Lightning and Sally were still waiting for their drinks when Lightning thought he heard Mater's voice on the TV in the background. Lightning didn't know it yet, but Mater was Mel's next caller.

"That I-talian fella you got on there can't talk that way about Lightning McQueen!" Mater shouted over the phone. His voice was broadcast loudly over the television set. "He's the bestest race car in the whole wide world."

Francesco smugly replied, "If he is, as you say, 'the bestest race car,' then why must he rest?"

A crowd was forming at the bar now. Everyone listened as Mater said, "'Cause he knows what's important! Every now and then he just prefers to slow down and enjoy life."

"You heard it," Francesco announced, gloating. "Lightning McQueen prefers to be slow. This is not news to Francesco. When I want to go to sleep, I watch one of his races. After two laps, I am out cold."

The Radiator Springs crowd began to boo. Sally and Lightning moved from their table to see what the commotion was about.

"Lightning McQueen is afraid of Francesco!" Francesco said, smiling. "This is understandable."

"Francesco Bernoulli," Sally said, admiring the Italian race car. "No wonder there's a crowd."

"How do you know his name? And don't say it like that: *Francessssco*," Lightning said, pouting. "It's three syllables, not ten!"

"What?" Sally said, still staring at the TV screen. "He's nice to look at—open-wheeled and all."

But Mater wasn't done with Francesco yet. "Lightning could drive circles around you!"

"Mel, can we move on?" The arrogant Francesco rudely interrupted Mater. "Francesco needs a caller who can provide a little more intellectual stimulation. Like a dump truck."

Now, that upset Lightning. The national racing champion headed to the phone.

"This is Lightning McQueen," Lightning said over the phone. "Look, I don't appreciate my best friend being insulted."

"Lightning, that was your best friend?" Francesco laughed. "This is the difference between you and Francesco. Francesco knows he is superior to others. He does not need to surround himself with bumpkins to prove it."

"Those are strong words from such a fragile car!" Lightning countered.

The conversation got more and more heated until Sir Miles Axlerod interrupted.

"This sounds like something that needs to be settled on the course," Sir Miles said. "What do you say, Lightning? I've got room for one more racer."

Lightning paused. He had let his pit crew go on vacation. He couldn't race without them! Suddenly, he looked around the room. He had a pit crew right there: Fillmore, Sarge, Luigi, and Guido.

"Yeah," Lightning announced to Axlerod and all the TV viewers around the world. "I'm in!"

Lightning turned to Sally. "I know," he apologized. "But we won't be long, and—"

"Don't worry about me." Sally stopped him gently. "But you're bringing Mater, right?" Then she added, "Just let him sit in the pits, give him a headset—thrill of a lifetime for him." She knew how much this would mean to Mater—and Lightning would need a good friend to support him in this big competition.

Lightning paused. Mater rolled over to them, bringing their drinks.

"How'd you like to come see the world with me?" Lightning asked Mater.

"Oh, yeah. They owe me a lot of vacation time," Mater replied, then let out a shriek of joy. "I'm in!" he shouted.

5

Lightning's new pit crew worked day and night to get him ready for the race. Ramone even gave him a new paint job with some special airbrushing. The finishing touch was a set of blinding new headlights. The World Grand Prix would not be run on traditional racetracks. The cars would race through city streets and countryside in Tokyo, Japan; Porto Corsa, Italy; and London, England. Lightning would need lights to race.

Of course, Guido and Luigi gave him new tires and packed several extra sets.

It wasn't long before Mater, Lightning, and his Radiator Springs pit crew rolled onto an airplane. They were on their way to Japan. Tokyo was the first leg of the three-part World Grand Prix race.

Mater enjoyed the free snacks and videos on the plane, but they were nothing compared to the bright and colorful lights of Tokyo. As they left the Tokyo airport, Mater was amazed by the city. He wanted to see and do everything.

As soon as they arrived in the heart of the city, Team Lightning McQueen went to see kabuki theater and sumo wrestling. Mater even joined in the fun by wearing kabuki face paint.

Later, they attended an official prerace party hosted by Sir Miles Axlerod. Lightning McQueen rolled up on the red carpet as the media cars crowded around for pictures. Mater had never seen anything like it in his life.

The party was held in an ultramodern museum with a huge indoor waterfall. All the car-racing greats were there, including Francesco.

"Mater, I'm so glad you got me into this thing," Lightning said as he spotted some of his racing friends.

"Me too, buddy!" Mater's eyes grew wide as he looked around at the fancy party. "Hey, what's that?" Mater started to drive away.

"No! Mater!" Lightning shouted too late. He was hoping desperately to keep his friend by his side. The rusty tow truck was not used to life outside Radiator Springs. He was bound to get into some sort of trouble.

But one of Lightning's racing pals pulled him into a conversation as Mater wandered off. A minute later, as they were talking, Lightning realized that a number of partygoers were looking at Mater and giggling.

"Who brought that guy?" Jeff Gorvette, another American race car, asked Lightning.

Mater was looking at a very serious car raking a rock garden with absolute precision, an old Japanese tradition. But Mater thought he was trying to rake leaves!

"Hey!" Mater shouted. "You done good! You got all the leaves!"

Lightning quickly rolled up to Mater and pulled him aside.

"Listen," Lightning whispered. "This isn't Radiator Springs." But Mater didn't seem to understand that he was embarrassing himself and Lightning! "I'm saying things are different over here," Lightning added. "Just help me out here, Mater."

Mater lit up like a bulb. "You need help? Shoot! Why didn't you say so? That's what a tow truck does."

They were suddenly distracted by the sound of

laughter across the room. Francesco Bernoulli was shamelessly flirting with some of the ladies.

"Hey, looky there," Mater said, glancing over at Francesco. "It's Mr. San Francisco!"

"Mater, wait!" Lightning said, but Mater drove off.

"Look at me!" Mater exclaimed. "I'm helping already!"

Lightning quickly followed Mater, hoping to bring him back. But it was too late. Mater had reached Francesco and begun the introductions.

"Hey, Mr. San Francisco," Mater said, addressing Francesco, "I'd like you to meet—"

"Lightning McQueen!" Francesco replied, looking Lightning up and down. *"Buona sera!"*

"Excuse me," Mater said, interrupting Francesco. "Can I get a picture with you? Miss Sally's gonna flip when she sees this. She's Lightning McQueen's girlfriend. She's a big fan of yours."

Francesco shrugged. "She has good taste."

Lightning tried to smile. "Mater's prone to exaggeration. I wouldn't say she's a *big* fan."

"You're right." Mater nodded. "She's a *huge* fan."

"Francesco is familiar with this reaction to Francesco." The Italian race car smiled, then added,

"I dedicate my win tomorrow to Miss Sally."

"Oh, sorry," Lightning replied. "I already dedicated my win tomorrow to her. So if we both do it, it's not really that special." Then, noticing Mater driving off toward more trouble, he added, "See you at the race!"

Francesco smiled. "Yes, you will see Francesco. But not like this," he said, gesturing smugly to his handsome face. Francesco turned and showed Lightning his rear bumper. It had a license plate that read CIAO, LIGHTNING MCQUEEN!

"That's cute," Lightning said. "You had one of those made up for all the racers?"

"No," Francesco said simply.

Lightning tried to shrug off his bad feeling as he rolled away. Francesco was making this race personal!

Meanwhile, as Sir Miles Axlerod told the media about the wonders of his new fuel, Allinol, a bank of cameras recorded every word. Several of the cameras displayed the letters WGP—just like the camera Professor Z had unwrapped on the oil derrick.

And, unobserved, Finn McMissile was checking them all out.

6

Hidden from the party guests, Finn McMissile was secretly running the image of every one of those WGP cameras through his computer. So far, each one had been rejected as NOT A MATCH with the camera from the oil derrick.

From out of the crowd, a gorgeous sports car parked herself next to Finn and swiftly eyed her surroundings. Then she leaned in and whispered the secret code, "A Volkswagen Karmann Ghia has no radiator."

Finn barely moved as he whispered the coded reply, "That's because it's air-cooled."

The two spies had been given the coded prompt and reply so that they could identify each other at this party. Now they moved swiftly into their hushed introductions.

"I'm Agent Shiftwell. Holley Shiftwell from the

Tokyo station," she said. "I have a message from London." Holley was a recent graduate of the secret-agent academy, brand-new to the world of espionage. Not a field agent like Finn, she did diagnostics work, examining and interpreting data.

"Not here," Finn whispered as he led Holley to a glass elevator. When the doors closed, he spoke more freely. "So the lab boys analyzed the photos I sent? What did they learn about that camera?"

"Nothing out of the ordinary, I'm afraid," Agent Shiftwell replied brusquely. "They said perhaps you could get closer pictures next time?"

Finn bristled. "A good spy gets what he can, then gets out before he's killed."

The younger agent looked flustered. "Yes, sir. Of course." Then she added, "There's an American agent who's been under deep cover on that oil platform. He was able to get a photo of the car who's running the entire operation."

"This could solve everything," Finn muttered.

"The American is here tonight to pass the photo to you," Holley added. "He'll signal you when he's ready."

Ding! The elevator doors swung open.

Finn was pleased with Holley's news. "Whoever's

in that photo is up to something big," he commented quietly. "He has hundreds of hooligans working for him, including Professor Z."

Holley, too, knew of Professor Z: "One of the most dangerous weapons designers in the world," she whispered. Then she added, "There's one other thing before I go: The oil field itself? It turns out it's the largest oil reserve in the world."

Finn pondered that for a moment. "This is bigger than I—" He stopped abruptly as he saw two Gremlins and a Pacer moving through the crowd—Professor Z's cars! Finn immediately recognized them from the oil derrick. He ducked behind a large Japanese ceremonial helmet. He knew that now he'd never be able to make contact with the American agent without being recognized.

"What is it?" Holley asked him.

"New plan," Finn told her swiftly. "*You're* meeting the American."

Mater continued to roll happily through the party. He really was beginning to feel at home in his glamorous new surroundings.

Wandering up to a sushi bar, he stared eagerly at the feast before him.

"Lightning's probably starving," he said to himself thoughtfully. Then he asked the chef, "Hey, you got anything that's free?"

Mater noticed the fiery-hot green wasabi. "What about that pistachio ice cream?"

"No, no, wasabi," the chef said, correcting him.

But Mater didn't understand. He still thought it was ice cream!

He pointed to the spicy green wasabi again. "That looks delicious. I should probably sample some myself just to be sure."

The chef nodded and put a small dab of wasabi aside for Mater. "Uh, a little more, please," Mater asked. The sushi chef's eyes widened as Mater asked for more and more.

"My condolences," the sushi chef said in Japanese when Mater finally drove off into the crowd with a huge glob of the hot green sauce.

As the party guests enjoyed their refreshments, Sir Miles Axlerod introduced Number 95, Lightning McQueen. The room erupted in cheers.

"You and your team bring excellence and

professionalism to the competition," Sir Miles was saying, when he was silenced by a piercing scream. It was Mater, driving in circles, eyes bloodshot red.

Mater peeled off toward the waterfall behind Lightning and Axlerod—and dove into the fountain.

"Sweet relief!" the tow truck howled as the water cooled his burning grille.

Sir Miles Axlerod was shocked. Lightning cringed. He could see that Mater was making a spectacle of himself. Other cars were laughing.

"Whatever you do, *do not* eat the free pistachio ice cream! It has turned!" Mater shouted. He was still splashing in the water and gasping for air. That hot green wasabi felt worse than an overheated radiator! Lightning turned to Axlerod and tried to apologize. "I can explain, Sir Miles," he said as he introduced Mater. "He's, uh, just a little excited."

"I can see that," Axlerod said, looking down at the floor between them.

Lightning looked down, too, and saw a puddle of oil. Mater had leaked!

"Mater!" Lightning whispered as he pulled him aside. "You have got to get ahold of yourself. You're making a scene!"

Mater was confused and embarrassed. "But I never leak oil," he told Lightning honestly.

Lightning just shook his head. "Go take care of yourself right now!"

Mater rushed through the crowd. "Comin' through," he said. "Where's the bathroom?"

7

Poor Mater found his way to the bathrooms, but the signs above the doors were in Japanese. Mater knew he had a fifty-fifty chance of getting it right. He made his choice and rolled in. Two seconds later he zipped out with the sound of high-pitched shrieking behind him.

"Sorry, ladies!" Mater called back.

Mater entered the ultramodern men's room. He rolled into an open stall and was very impressed. It was equipped with a fancy lift and a flat-screen monitor.

Mater pushed a few buttons. Lights began flashing. The little stall seemed to come alive with moving gadgets, and the monitor lit up.

"Welcome to the bathroom!" a little cartoon character giggled. Mater wasn't sure if he should hide. The character was a girl!

Now, *this* was something Mater had never experienced! The lift began to rise under him as the little character said, "Please sit quietly and let us do the work for you."

A tiny spurt of water tickled him. Mater giggled.

Then Mater screamed! The water flow had increased, shooting up into his undercarriage. The water was freezing! Gadgets from every direction began poking and prodding him. Mater desperately pressed knobs and buttons, adjusting water velocity, temperature, and brushes. A lot of things were working, all right, but none of them was doing what Mater wanted! He just wanted to leave!

Outside Mater's stall, Rod Redline, the American agent, was getting ready to pass off the information he had for Finn. He removed his disguise and looked at himself in the mirror.

"Okay, McMissile," he muttered under his breath. "I'm here. It's time to make the drop."

Swiftly, Rod sent out a coded signal to Finn.

Immediately Holley picked it up. "The American has activated his tracking beacon," she radioed Finn, waiting for further instructions from him.

"Roger that," Finn replied. Then the seasoned

British agent told Holley, "Okay, move in."

As Holley rolled toward the men's room, Mater slammed buttons and thrashed about, struggling to get out of the stall.

Just outside, Grem and Acer had discovered Rod. The American agent had been cornered and barely stood a chance against Professor Z's two thugs. They fought as Mater thrashed around inside the stall.

Finally, Mater crashed through the stall door, smashing into the thugs.

Mater had no idea that he had just interrupted a brawl. Rod was already pretty badly beaten. Professor Z's two cars were determined to recover his top-secret information.

Huffing and puffing, Mater stared at Grem and Acer. He towed cars like these all the time back home in Radiator Springs!

"Hey! A Gremlin and a Pacer! No offense to your makes and models, but you guys break down harder than—" Mater stopped short. He felt a tickle as Rod slipped a small device into his undercarriage.

"What the . . . ?" Mater said as he turned and saw Rod for the first time. "Whoa. You okay?" Mater asked the battered American agent.

"I'm fine," Rod responded, knowing that Grem and Acer wouldn't get the information he'd been carrying. It would soon be out the door with this dented old tow truck. The device he'd slipped into Mater's undercarriage contained information that would lead Agent McMissile to the head of Professor Z's evil operation.

"Hey, tow truck?" Grem said, trying to get Mater's attention. "We'd like to get to our *private business* here, if you don't mind."

"Oh, yeah, sorry," Mater answered. "Don't let me get in the way of your private business." He was about to leave, then turned back and added, "Oh! A little advice: When you hear her giggle, press that green button. It's to adjust the temperature."

"Got it," Acer answered.

"All right, then," Mater said, and rolled out of the bathroom.

With Mater gone, Grem and Acer turned their attention back to Rod.

Outside the men's room door, Holley picked up the signal coming from the device on Mater. The rusty, dented tow truck was hardly keeping a low profile.

"This can't be him," she said into her radio. No

secret agent she'd ever heard of would act like this!

Mater was shaking a rear tire as he approached the dance floor. "Look out, ladies," he said. "Mater's fittin' to get funky."

"Is he American?" Finn radioed back.

Holley sighed. "Very."

"Then it's him," Finn told her.

Holley quickly drifted over to Mater and whispered the coded message: "A Volkswagen Karmann Ghia has no radiator."

"Of course it doesn't," Mater replied. "That's because it's air-cooled."

If there was anyone who knew all about cars, it was Mater. He was a tow truck, after all. He loved to help other cars. When they broke down, he tried to fix them or tow them. It was his nature.

In the world of espionage, though, Mater had just delivered a secret code to identify himself as an international spy! Naturally, Holley and Finn assumed he was the American agent.

"I'm from the Tokyo office," Holley began to tell him. But Mater wasn't done giving her all the facts on air-cooled engines. She was, after all, a very pretty car, and he was hoping to impress her.

He rattled on about all sorts of makes, models, and years in car history before Holley finally interrupted.

"Listen," she said, "we should find somewhere more private. Impossible to know which areas here are compromised. When can I see you again?"

"Well, let's see," Mater answered happily. He couldn't believe she was asking him out on a date! "Tomorrow I'll be out there at the races."

"Got it," Holley replied. "We'll rendezvous then."

Mater strolled back to the party and finally met up with his team.

"There you are," Lightning said to him. "Where have you been?"

Mater seemed to be in a daze. "What's a 'rendezvous'?" he asked Luigi.

"It'sa like a date," Luigi answered.

"A date!" Mater said, thrilled.

"*Non ci credo!*" Guido answered.

Luigi translated. "Guido don't believe you."

"Well, believe it," Mater said to them proudly. "There she is right there." Mater nodded in the direction of the beautiful British sports car across the room. "Hey, hey, lady!" he shouted.

Holley glanced at Mater and quickly drove off. She did not want their cover to be blown!

"See you tomorrow," Mater called after her.

"Non ci credo," Guido said again. The little forklift kept shaking his head.

Luigi translated. "Guido still don't believe you."

Somewhere on an industrial dock in the city of Tokyo, Grem and Acer had Rod suspended from an electromagnet.

"I gotta admit: you tricked us real good," Grem said to Rod.

"And we don't like to be tricked," Acer snapped.

Rod simply smiled.

"Hey, what's so funny?" Acer demanded.

"Well," Rod said, embracing the fact that he was in serious trouble. "You know, *I* was just wearing a disguise. You guys are *stuck* looking like that." He knew he was about to be roughed up by these two thugs. He figured he could at least insult them first.

Rod steeled himself as he was lowered onto a treadmill. He guessed they would start by making him run until he stalled out. He could handle that, but he wasn't sure what other means they would use to get his secrets. A gas tank filled with Allinol stood next to him.

"Allinol?" Rod said. "Thanks, fellas. I hear this stuff is good for you."

"So you think!" The mood changed dramatically as Professor Z emerged from the darkness and addressed Rod. "Allinol by itself is good for you. But what poor Miles Axlerod doesn't know is that we've secretly sabotaged his wonder fuel. When hit with a blast of radiation, it becomes extremely dangerous."

Rod looked up and spotted the mysterious camera with WGP printed on its side—the same one Finn had seen earlier on the oil derrick. But this was no camera. A piercing beam of light suddenly shot from the lens.

"You were very interested in this camera on the oil platform," Professor Z said as he turned up the intensity of the beam. "Well, now you will witness what it really does."

"Whatever you say, Professor." Rod's engine, now filled with Allinol, began to heat up. He couldn't figure out why, but he could endure the pain. It was part of his training.

Grem and Acer turned on a video monitor in front of Rod. Footage of the prerace party flashed into view.

"You talked up a lot of cars last night. Which one is your 'associate'?" Acer demanded.

But Rod refused to answer.

Grem was beginning to get ticked off. "Should I start it, Professor?"

"Do fifty-percent power," Professor Z replied mildly. He turned to stare right into Rod's eyes. "This camera is actually an electromagnetic radiation emitter. The Allinol is now heating to a boil, dramatically expanding, causing the engine block to crack under stress, forcing oil into the combustion chamber."

"What do I care?" Rod grimaced. He could feel his engine beginning to give way. "I can replace an engine block."

"You may be able to," Professor Z said smugly. "But after full exposure to the radiation, unfortunately, there will be nothing to replace."

"How about him?" Acer asked, flashing some footage of Mater rolling out of the men's room. Professor Z noticed that it caught Rod's attention— he saw a split second of recognition in Rod's eyes.

"That's him. He's the one," Professor Z said as he stared at Mater's image on the TV monitor.

"No!" Rod protested.

But the Professor rolled away and radioed his mysterious leader, the Big Boss himself.

"Yes, sir," Professor Z said. "We believe the infiltrator has passed along sensitive information."

An angry voice replied over the radio: "Well, then, get it! You'd better make sure this doesn't get any further!"

"I will take care of it before any damage can be done," Professor Z quickly replied. There was a sharp click over the radio. The "leader" had turned off his radio. He—or she—had nothing more to say.

Professor Z turned toward Grem and Acer. "The project is still on schedule," he said. Then he ordered them to find Mater, the so-called second agent. Mater didn't know it, but his life was in danger!

Professor Z turned the camera beam to its highest setting. In seconds, there was a fiery explosion and Rod Redline was no more.

The first race of the World Grand Prix was held in nighttime Tokyo. The excitement and glitter were almost overwhelming. The announcer, Brent Mustangburger, was calling the action, along with David Hobbscapp and Darrell Cartrip in the studio.

"Welcome to the inaugural running of the World Grand Prix!" Brent said into his microphone. "David, how exactly does this competition work?"

"Brent, all three courses start with classic straightaways. Look for Francesco Bernoulli in particular to lead early."

"Whoa now, hold your horsepower! You're forgetting the most important factor here: that early dirt-track section of the course!" Darrell interrupted his fellow announcer. "Don't forget Lightning McQueen! His mentor, the Hudson Hornet, was one of the greatest dirt-track racers of all time! In my opinion, Lightning's the best all-round racer in this competition."

"Well, it's time to find out," Brent Mustangburger said, putting an end to the friendly banter. "The racers are locking into the grid!"

Down at the starting line, Lightning was in position, engine revving. His eyes shut tight as he focused mentally on the race.

"Speed. I. Am. Speed," Lightning whispered.

"You are speed?" Francesco interrupted. "Then Francesco must be triple speed."

Lightning opened his eyes at the irritating sound of Francesco's cocky voice. The flashy racer was lined up right next to Lightning.

"Francesco likes this, Lightning," Francesco continued. "It's really getting him in the zone."

"He is so getting beat today," Lightning muttered to himself, determined to win.

The starting lights clicked down from red to yellow to green. The race was on! Francesco sped out for a quick start, taking the lead.

"Hang on, boys!" Brent Mustangburger exclaimed.

Team Lightning McQueen was glued to the pit monitors—but no one more than Mater.

"Lightning!" Mater shouted into his headset as he saw the racers approach the dirt track. "Time to make your move. Get on the outside and show them what Doc done taught you."

"Ten-four, Mater," Lightning answered over his radio. He was glad to have his friend helping out.

Francesco, who was the first to hit the dirt section, suddenly skidded out of control and slammed to a stop. Lightning sped past him.

"Yeah! Nice call, Mater! Keep it up!" Lightning cried out, delighted to be in the lead.

Lightning picked up traction as he moved from the dirt section onto the city streets. The other racers passed Francesco as the pack made the final turns through the brightly lit downtown roads. They were quickly gaining on Lightning.

"As we head back through the city," Brent Mustangburger observed, "there's a whole lot of knockin' at Lightning McQueen's door." Brent took a breath. "As they finish lap one, the racers are practically even again!"

The racers shot past a tower under the eyes of Agents Finn McMissile and Holley Shiftwell. They were looking for the American agent with the information on Professor Z. It was Holley who spotted him first—in the Team Lightning McQueen pit.

Holley watched Mater carefully through her high-tech telescopic display.

"Why is he in the pits?" she asked Finn in dismay. "He's so exposed."

"It's his cover," Finn answered. "One of the best I've ever seen, too. Look at the detail on his rust. Must have cost a fortune."

Holley nodded. "Okay, then why hasn't he contacted us yet?"

"There's probably heat on him," Finn answered calmly. "He's clearly a seasoned veteran. He'll reach out when he's ready."

Finn scanned the World Grand Prix cameras, still looking for the fake one he had spotted with Professor Z and his thugs on the oil derrick. Finn had no idea what Professor Z had just done to the real agent, Rod, by using that fake WGP camera. But Finn McMissile did have good instincts.

In the shadows on another rooftop, Grem and Acer were placing Professor Z's camera in position.

"It is time," the Professor told them over a radio. "Start small, please."

"Roger that," Grem said as he angled the camera toward Miguel Camino. As soon as the radiation beam hit him, Miguel's engine began smoking.

"Oh!" Darrell Cartrip said into his microphone. "Miguel Camino has blown an engine."

"That's very unusual, Darrell," one of the announcers said. "He's been so consistent all year."

Grem watched the burned-out car roll into the pits. Then something caught his eye. "You gotta be kidding me," Grem said.

"What? What is it?" Acer asked him.

"It's that tow truck from the bathroom," Grem said, spotting Mater. "The one the American agent passed the device to. He's in the pits!"

"Not for long," Acer replied as the two took off in Mater's direction.

Holley picked up the movement right away. "I think I've got something," she said to Finn.

"The camera?" he asked anxiously.

"No," Holly replied.

10

Holly swiftly ran a computer check. Finally, she found the information she wanted: "The Pacer from the party last evening," she said to Finn. "I'm cross-referencing with the photos from the oil derrick. His VIN numbers match!"

Holley ran a search for known associates.

"Hang on," she said to Finn as the computer pulled up a long list—too long. "He's not the only one. Three . . . five . . . Gremlins and Pacers. They're everywhere! And they're all closing in on— Oh, no!" Holley gasped as Mater's smiling face filled her screen. She turned to tell Finn, but he was already gone.

The next time Holley heard Finn's voice, it was over her radio. He was dashing to intercept Professor Z's cars before they could get to Mater.

"Get him out of the pits!" Finn radioed Holley. "Now!" The situation was urgent.

Within minutes, Mater heard a voice coming through the radio crackle. "Can you hear me? Over?"

"Huh? What?" Mater answered.

"Get out of the pits now! Do you hear me?" Holley urged Mater, desperately trying to move him away from danger.

Mater grinned. It was the pretty car from last night's party! He had no idea who she really was!

Just then, another car suddenly began burning black smoke. It skidded off the track.

"Another blown engine!" the announcer said. "This is the second one tonight!"

Meanwhile, Mater had not budged from the Team Lightning McQueen pit.

"Get out now!" Holley repeated to him.

"All right, then," Mater replied, and turned to drive into the pit's access tunnel. "You know, I usually like to have a proper detailing done before I meet a lady friend."

As Mater moved through the tunnel, Finn intercepted Acer with another Pacer from the oil derrick. Acer recognized the British agent.

"Finn McMissile!" Acer cried. He and the other Pacers and Gremlins had thought the secret agent had disappeared forever after leaping off Professor Z's oil derrick.

Finn used the element of surprise to spray them with a fire extinguisher before speeding away. Blinded for only a second, the two Pacers zoomed after him.

Finn dashed to a side street. He needed to get a fix on Mater's location.

"Miss Shiftwell?" he called over his radio.

"I've got him in the back alleys east of the garages," she said as she stared at her computer monitor. "Multiple assailants are closing in quickly!"

"Keep him moving," Finn replied to Holley. "I'm on my way."

Mater bumbled around the backstreets of Tokyo, looking for his date. He was still wearing his headset for the racetrack.

"Hey, new lady friend?" he said into his radio. He had spotted a flower shop. "You like flowers?"

From the track, Lightning responded with a startled "What?" He had no idea that Holley had tapped into

Mater's headset. He could not hear Holley. He only heard Mater!

"No!" Holley said to Mater. "Don't go *in* anywhere."

"Stay outside. Gotcha," Mater radioed back.

"Outside?" Lightning asked. Trusting his buddy, he overrode his better judgment and cut to the outside of the track. It was just enough of an opening for Francesco to sail into the lead.

"*Grazie* and *arrivederci!*" Francesco said as he sped past Lightning. Lightning groaned in disbelief. Why had Mater told him to stay outside?

"I can't believe what I just saw!" Darrell Cartrip said to Brent Mustangburger. "You don't open up the inside like that!"

"And it just might have cost Lightning McQueen first place," Brent said.

Meanwhile, in the back alleys of Tokyo, Finn was still trying to divert Professor Z's cars away from Mater. But a gang of Pacers was herding Finn in Acer's direction. They were trying to surround him! Acer still had some fire retardant on him, but this time he wasn't going to be surprised by Finn McMissile. He had a flamethrower ready.

Mater passed the entrance to an alley. He heard the commotion and saw some flames.

"You're doing fine," Holley told Mater, trying to keep him away. "Just stay focused."

But Mater headed toward Finn and the enemy cars. He wanted to see what was happening.

"No!" Holley shouted. "Don't go down that street!"

Mater showed up just in time to see Finn leap forward and attack Professor Z's cars with his world-class martial arts moves.

"Wow! A karate demonstration!" Mater shouted in delight. He was so excited that he forgot he was on the radio with both Holley *and Lightning!*

Lightning heard Mater's exclamation down on the track. "I've had enough of this, Mater. Just sign off."

Mater didn't even hear Lightning. He wanted to get the karate expert's autograph. But before he knew it, the guy was gone.

"Where'd he go?" Mater asked, looking around.

Just then Holley said, "Our rendezvous has been jeopardized. Keep the device safe. We'll be in touch."

"Dadgum!" Mater said. "Did I miss our date?"

It was like a bad dream for Lightning McQueen. Francesco Bernoulli was on the media stage, gloating about his victory.

"Francesco!" the adoring reporters cried. "What was your strategy today?"

"Francesco's strategy was very simple," Francesco said as he smiled for the cameras. "Start the race. Wait for Lightning McQueen to choke. Pass him. Win. Francesco always wins. It's boring."

Lightning was on a side stage, doing a slow burn. Then he spotted Mater. The dented tow truck was looking around, confused.

"Oh, hey, Lightning! What happened?" he asked. "Is the race over? You won, right?"

"Mater, why were you yelling those things at me while I was racing?" Lightning sputtered.

Mater shrugged. "Yelling? Oh, you thought I was talkin' to you? That's funny right there. No, see that's 'cause I saw these two fellers doing some kind of karate street performance! It was nutso. One of them even had a flamethrower!"

"A flamethrower!" Lightning exclaimed. "Mater, I don't understand. Where were you?"

"Going to meet my date," Mater said, still not understanding what he'd done—until he saw the look on Lightning's face.

"I lost the race because of you!" Lightning shouted angrily at his friend. "This is exactly why I don't bring you along to these things!"

Mater was stunned. "I'm sorry. I didn't mean to. Maybe if I—I dunno—talked to somebody and explained what happened, it could help."

"I don't need your help!" Lightning snapped as the media began to pull him away for interviews. "I don't *want* your help!"

Mater was pushed backward as the reporters swarmed Lightning. He hovered for a few minutes while he listened to Lightning talking to them.

"I made a mistake," Lightning said, "but I can assure you, it won't happen again in the next race."

Mater was sure he was the mistake Lightning was talking about. He decided there was only one thing to do. He would go back to Radiator Springs and let Lightning race his own way. He didn't want to hurt his friend's chances of winning the next two races.

On Lightning's pit monitor, the postrace commentary continued.

"To recap," Brent Mustangburger said, "Lightning McQueen loses in the last lap to Francesco Bernoulli. And three, count 'em, three cars flamed out, leading some to suggest that their fuel, Allinol, might be to blame."

The cameras switched live to Sir Miles Axlerod. He was trying to defend his new fuel to the media.

"Allinol is safe!" he insisted.

The announcer, Darrell Cartrip, looked doubtful. "Well, the jury may still be out on whether Allinol caused these accidents, but one thing's for sure: Lightning McQueen blew this race."

Mater saw the postrace show from a monitor at the Tokyo airport. Sadly, he headed toward the gates, knowing he'd let his best buddy down.

Mater never noticed Grem and Acer following him. A security guard suddenly approached Mater.

"Come with me, please, sir," the security guard said, escorting Mater around a corner.

"But I'm gonna miss my plane!" Mater protested.

The security guard dropped his disguise. He was Finn McMissile.

"Hey, I know you!" Mater said excitedly. "You're that fella from the karate demonstration!"

They entered a private lounge. "I never properly introduced myself," Finn said. "Finn McMissile. British intelligence."

Mater grinned. He didn't understand Finn's phrase. "Tow Mater," he said. "Average intelligence."

"Who are you with?" Finn asked. "FBI? CIA?"

"Let's just say I'm Triple-A-affiliated," Mater said.

Finn eyed Mater for a moment. Then Mater took a karate stance. "Don't wanna brag or nothin', but I've got me a black fan belt. You wanna see some moves I made up?"

As Mater clumsily kicked and chopped at the air, Finn noticed Grem and Acer right outside the lounge.

"There he is!" Grem shouted, pointing at Mater.

Quickly, Finn cut a perfect circle in the window that overlooked the tarmac.

Then he hooked Mater. "Hang on!"

Finn leaped straight through the glass, taking Mater with him. The fallen piece of glass created a smooth ramp to the airport runway. Finn pulled Mater down hard when they reached the tarmac and zipped him away from the terminal building.

"Whoa!" a delighted Mater shouted at the top of his lungs. "This is first-class service! You don't even have to go through the terminal!"

But Acer and Grem were right behind them. "Drive forward," Finn told Mater sharply. "Whatever you do, don't stop."

Finn skidded around so that now Mater was towing him. Finn faced Grem, ready for the attack. Before he hit the tarmac, Grem managed to fire a rocket. Finn intercepted it with a rocket of his own.

Ka-blam!

"Everything okay back there?" Mater asked.

Just then, Siddeley, a British spy jet, appeared overhead, engines roaring.

"Finn," the jet radioed, "It's Sid. I'm on approach."

"Roger that," Finn replied.

Up ahead, Acer appeared on the tarmac. He was dragging a long row of luggage carts. Mater and Finn were going to run right into the baggage train!

Fillmore, Luigi, Guido, and Mater
help out in the pits.

Lightning McQueen is not only one of the fastest
race cars in the world, but also Mater's best buddy.

Finn McMissile is a British secret agent.

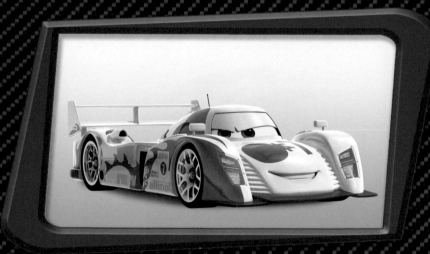

Japan's favorite racing marvel is Shu Todoroki.

Francesco Bernoulli, the international racing sensation, loves to talk about himself.

Secret agent Holley Shiftwell accidentally ends up on her first big assignment with Finn McMissile.

Mater goes to the World Grand Prix with Lightning McQueen and gets mistaken for an American spy!

Professor Z commands a group of cars, called Lemons, who break down a lot.

Uncle Topolino is Luigi's wise relative and the head of his extended family.

Tomber is a spare-parts dealer who works in Paris.

The secret-agent jet, Siddeley, loves to fly!

Professor Z and his Lemon helper test
the destructive power of their WGP "camera."

Professor Z's Lemon thugs, Grem and Acer,
prepare for a brawl.

Tire expert Luigi loves traveling to Italy
to see all his relatives.

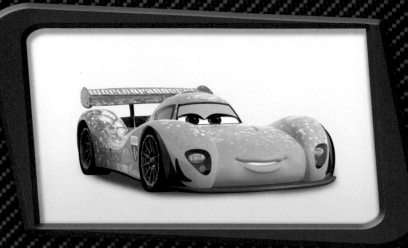

Carla Veloso is the pride of Brazil.
She specializes in endurance racing.

Though he loves his headquarters in Radiator Springs,
Lightning McQueen gets a charge out of racing
on different tracks around the world!

Siddeley the jet swept down and blew the luggage carts apart.

"Ahhhhhhhhhh!" Mater howled as the luggage exploded. "I knew I should've done carry-on!"

And in one swift move, Finn drove toward the jet, pulling Mater after him.

"Thanks, old boy!" Finn said to Siddeley.

"You got it, mate!" Siddeley replied. He pulled his rear cargo door down for Mater and Finn to board. Holley was waiting inside.

Mater smiled. "Hey! Doggone it, look! It's my imaginary girlfriend!"

At that same moment, in his suite at a Tokyo hotel, Lightning McQueen was looking at the goodbye note Mater had left behind. Guido, Luigi, Sarge, and Fillmore were at Lightning's side as he tried to read Mater's handwriting:

I don't want to be the cause of you losing any more races. I want you to prove to the world what I already know—that you are the greatest race car in the whole wide world. Your best friend, Mater.

Lightning handed the note to Luigi and turned away for a moment.

"I didn't really want him to leave," Lightning said to himself with mixed emotions. "Well, at least I know he's at home and he'll be okay."

But Mater wasn't on a commercial jet heading for home. High above them, Mater was gaining altitude on board Siddeley, the high-speed, high-tech, tough-as-nails British spy jet.

"Hey, do you guys know if this is a nonstop to Radiator Springs?" Mater asked Finn and Holley.

Holley used her electronic scanner on Mater and located the device the American agent had planted on him. A robotic arm shot out of her computer and yanked the device from under Mater's rear bumper.

"Yow!" Mater shouted. "I gotta go to a doctor. I keep getting these sharp pains in my undercarriage!"

Then Mater remembered his manners. "Lemme introduce you two. This here is Finn McSomething-or-other. He's a first-class airport watchamacallit. And Finn, this here's my date." Mater turned to Holley. "I never did get your name."

Holley hardly looked up from her work as she replied, "Shiftwell. Holley Shiftwell."

Mater turned back to Finn to finish the introductions. "It's Shiftwell. Holley—"

Suddenly, Holley drew up an image on her computer monitor.

"Finally," Finn said, eager to see the information from the American agent's recording device. "Time to see who's behind all this."

The computer suddenly projected a holographic image between Mater and Holley. It showed the details of a car engine.

"What is this, Mater?" Finn asked.

Mater looked at the image and shrugged. "That? That's easy. That's one of the worst engines ever made. It's an old aluminum V-8 engine with a Lucas electrical system and Whitworth bolts!" Mater explained that Whitworth bolts were a pain to get off. Every good mechanic knew that.

"Whose engine is this, Mater?" Finn asked.

"It's kinda hard to tell from this picture, ain't it?" Mater answered.

Holley stared at Mater. "But you're the one who took it!" Then she looked at Finn. "Oh, of course," she added. "A good spy gets what he can, then gets out before he's killed."

"You guys is spies?" Mater was dumbfounded.

Finn turned and looked at Holley. "This was supposed to be a photo of the car behind everything— not just his engine!"

Holley searched for more information, but there was only that single image.

"An engine like this could be in any number of cars," Finn said, thinking aloud. "This doesn't help us at all. It's a dead end. I am not happy about this."

"You might not be, but *he's* gotta be," Mater commented.

Finn was getting increasingly frustrated. "Who are you talking about?"

"This clunker here," Mater said simply as he looked more closely at the engine in the image. "See how he's had most of his parts replaced? Those are original parts. They aren't easy to come by."

"Rare parts," Holley said to Finn. "That's something we can track."

"Well done, Mater!" Finn exclaimed. "I never would have seen that. I know a black-market parts dealer in Paris. He's a treacherous lowlife, but he's the only car in the world who can tell us whose engine this is. Mater, what would you say to forming an informal task force on this one?"

"Well," Mater answered hesitantly, "okay. But you know I'm just a tow truck, right?"

"Right. And I'm just in the import-export business!" Finn winked at Mater and Holley. Then he called to Siddeley: "Paris, *toute suite!*"

"Yeah, two of them sweets for me, too, Sid!" Mater shouted. "You know, I always wanted to be a spy."

13

As Siddeley reached cruising altitude, he asked Finn, "Afterburners, sir?"

"Is there any other way?" Finn replied.

The jet suddenly jolted forward, and in a few short hours they were looking down at Paris.

Once they'd landed, Mater carefully followed Finn and Holley through backstreets and along alleys toward Finn's "contact." Mater was excited to see the sights, but he tried extra hard to follow Finn and Holley's lead. This was serious business!

They soon reached a marketplace where cars swarmed them, speaking in French. It seemed that every car had something to sell!

Just then a wobbly three-wheeled car turned in their direction and spotted Finn.

Tomber was a parts dealer who drove a hard

bargain. He also was Finn's informant. But Tomber didn't like strangers or his customers to know he had a relationship with the law. So when he saw Finn with a tow truck, he took off like a shot.

Finn finally caught up with him. "Mater! This chap's double-parked. You know what to do."

Mater's tow hook shot out like a whip. Moments later, Mater was towing Tomber into a dark garage. Holly followed as Finn quickly pulled the door shut, so the four cars could speak in private.

It was all part of the game. Tomber could not afford to let the crowd outside see him talking with strange cars. Finn was pretending to kidnap him while he actually gathered information.

Holley whipped out the holographic photo of the bad engine identified by Mater.

"All right, informant," Holley said. "Inform us."

"What a bucket of bolts!" Tomber exclaimed. "Wait. The parts: original from the manufacturer."

"Any idea who this might be?" Finn probed.

"I haven't seen parts like this in years. They're very rare and very expensive," Tomber said, confirming Mater's previous remarks. He paused and added, "I'm sorry, Finn. I can't help you."

"Mater, is there anything else you can tell us about this engine?" Holley asked desperately.

"Sorry." Mater frowned. "I told you everything I know about this Lemon."

Everyone in the room paused.

"Lemon?" Holley asked.

"Yeah, you know—cars that don't work right," Mater replied. "Lemons are a tow truck's bread and butter. Like those Pacers and Gremlins at the party and race and airport and such? They're Lemons, too."

"Holley," Finn blurted. "Pull up the pictures I took on the oil platform. I want to know what other types of cars were out there."

Holley pulled up the photos and started naming the cars. "There were some Hugos."

"Mater, is a Hugo considered a Lemon?" Finn asked. He was detecting a trend!

Mater chuckled. A Hugo was definitely a Lemon. And so were the Trunkovs Holley identified in the photos from the oil derrick. Even the genius mastermind Professor Z was a Lemon!

"Finn," Holley commented, "every car involved in this plot is one of history's biggest loser cars. And they're all taking their orders from whoever this is." Once again she brought up the image of the mysterious and poorly constructed engine.

"Life made him a Lemon," Finn said, musing aloud. "So he made Lemons his aid."

Tomber's eyes grew wide. This was familiar! "This explains it!" he announced. "There've been rumors of a secret meeting of these so-called Lemon cars in Porto Corsa in two days."

"Then there's a good chance *he'll* be there, too." Finn smiled as an idea formed in his mind. Quickly, he told Holley to contact their bullet train. They were heading to Porto Corsa!

Mater's eyes lit up. "Hey, if we're gonna be near the next race, maybe we could swing by the pits, and you could tell Lightning how much I'm helping!"

"Tell Lightning what?" Holley looked confused.

But Finn was focused on the Lemons and their upcoming meeting. Now he had a plan: the secret agents would travel to Italy and infiltrate that meeting. Perhaps that would be where they would find out who was behind this plot—and why.

Meanwhile, the race cars and their teams were on their way to the same place as Mater and the two agents, but with different plans and expectations. In Porto Corsa, the small town on the sunny coast of Italy, everyone was excitedly preparing for the second race of the WGP. Lightning and his crew—Luigi, Guido, Sarge, and Fillmore— had just arrived in their WGP transport vehicle.

Porto Corsa also happened to be near the hometown of Luigi and Guido. The cousins couldn't have been more delighted.

"Guido!" Luigi said as they rolled into the town's piazza. "Your eyes do not deceive you. We are home!"

Fillmore got out of the transport and looked around. "Luigi, which way to the hotel?"

"What?" Luigi said quickly. "No friends of mine will stay in a hotel in my country. You will stay with my Uncle Topolino!"

14

As Team Lightning McQueen approached the Maserati fountain in the center of town, a 1937 Fiat rolled into the piazza. It was Uncle Topolino! The piazza soon filled with all of Guido and Luigi's Fiat family. Tears of joy were flowing as fast as the water in the fountain.

Everyone was smiling. But Uncle Topolino noticed Lightning out of the corner of his eye.

"Race car," the wise older car said to Lightning. "You look so down. So low. It's like you have flat tires."

"He's clearly starving," Mamma Topolino said. "I'ma gonna make him a big meal right now, fatten him up." Lightning tried to stop her, but Mamma rolled away toward the kitchen.

Uncle Topolino took Lightning aside. "I

understand," he said. "Is a problem, yes? Between you and a friend?"

"How'd you know that?" Lightning asked, impressed.

Uncle Topolino shrugged and replied simply: "A wise car hears one word and understands two. That, and Luigi told me. While Mamma cooks, come and take a stroll with me."

It was hard for Lightning to talk about, but finally he said, "Mater made me lose the race, we had a huge fight, and he ended up going home." Lightning paused and added: "It's for the best, though."

"Best for him? Or for you?" the older car asked.

Lightning was startled. "What do you mean?"

"This Mater is a close friend?"

"He's my best friend," Lightning replied.

Uncle Topolino rolled slowly forward. "Then why would you want him to be someone else?"

Lightning considered this for a moment. Lightning now understood that he needed to accept Mater for exactly who he was. Mater was his best friend!

Uncle Topolino gazed into the piazza. Party lights were twinkling, and the sound of music was everywhere. "You know, back when Guido and Luigi worked for me, they would fight over everything."

Lightning could see Luigi dancing with a lady Fiat—and then he saw Guido suddenly cut in.

Uncle Topolino continued. "So I tell them: *'Va bene.'* It's okay to fight. Everybody fights now and then, especially best friends."

They watched Luigi cut back in on Guido. Finally Guido and Luigi danced together with the lady and her girlfriend.

"But you gotta make up fast," Uncle Topolino added. "No fight is more important than a friendship. Whoever finds a friend, finds a treasure."

Lightning sighed. He knew it was good advice.

Mamma Topolino returned with a huge platter and scolded, "Now eat!"

Lightning didn't know that at that moment Mater was traveling in a supersleek spy train on his way to Porto Corsa. Along with Finn and Holley, Mater was looking at surveillance photos of traffic in the little Italian town.

Finn was very impressed with Mater's knowledge of car makes and models.

"That one's a Gremlin. There's another Lemon right there," Mater was saying as he scanned the photos of Porto Corsa. "That three-wheeled feller had to be right about a big meeting. You never see this many Lemons in one town."

They took a look at a perfectly maintained Hugo being towed by an Eastern European tow truck.

"Must be one of the heads of the Lemon families," Finn said. "That's why he's in such pristine condition. We've got to find a way to infiltrate that meeting and find out who's behind all this."

"Hold on," Holley said as she snapped a photo of Mater. She turned back to her computer and superimposed an image of the European tow truck over Mater. It would be the perfect disguise. Mater could be the one to infiltrate the meeting!

"Good job, Miss Shiftwell!" Finn said, liking the idea.

Mater had no idea what was going on. He was still blinking from the camera flash.

"Wait, what's the plan?" he asked.

But Finn and Holley did not reply. They simply stared at Mater, looking for flaws in the disguise. As the spy train screamed through the darkness,

Holley worked on outfitting Mater for his mission. After adding the finishing touches, she fastened a tiny device behind the emergency light on his roof.

"That should just about do it," she said.

"Perfect," Finn said to Holley.

Mater looked in his side mirrors. He didn't notice anything different. He was still the same old dented red tow truck he'd always been.

"So, Mater," Holley said, "it's voice-activated. But, you know, everything's voice-activated these days."

"What?" Mater asked. "I thought you were supposed to be making me a disguise."

Instantly, a computerized voice responded: "Voice recognized. Disguise program initiated."

At the sound of Mater's voice, a holographic image suddenly spiraled out from the device on his roof. The device dropped the cloaking image of the sleek European tow truck right over Mater's body.

"Cool!" Mater exclaimed when he looked into his side mirrors again. "Hey, computer!" he called out. "Make me a German truck!"

Mater was delighted to suddenly see himself transformed into a German model.

"Make me a monster truck!" Mater said, loving this

new gadget. "A funny car!" he said next, laughing.

The computer easily rotated through Mater's commands. Holley rolled her eyes and switched it back to the European tow truck. Mater frowned. He was having fun and didn't want to stop!

"The idea is to keep a low profile," Finn reminded him politely but firmly.

15

"**S**o I just go in and pretend to be this tow truck?" Mater asked anxiously.

"And leave the rest to us," Holley answered as she deployed a bond sprayer to fill Mater's dents.

Mater suddenly pulled away. "Hey, what are you doing?" Then he took a breath. "For a second I thought you were trying to fix my dents."

"I was," Holley replied.

Mater straightened up. "Well then, no thank you. I don't get those dents buffed, pulled, filled, or painted by nobody. They're way too valuable."

Holley seemed surprised. "Your dents are valuable? Really?" she asked.

"I came by each one of them with my best friend, Lightning McQueen. I don't fix these. I want to remember these dents forever."

"Friendships can be dangerous in our line of work," Finn said to him.

"But my line of work is towing and salvage," Mater answered. He was *supposed* to be friendly!

Finn laughed, admiring Mater's brilliant cover. "Right!" Finn said, chuckling.

Mater frowned. "No, I meant that for real. I—"

"No, no. It's okay." Holley stopped Mater. "Say no more. I'll work around the dent."

"In the meantime, you look a little light on weapons," Finn said as the spy train began its descent into Italy. Mater brightened right up when Finn hit a button and an entire wall of the train transformed into a huge store of gleaming high-tech weaponry.

In the sunny town of Porto Corsa, fans from all over the world gathered to watch the second race of the WGP. Luxurious yachts dotted the sparkling harbor, and expensive shops had their doors open ready to greet them.

The town's winding roads had been converted into a racecourse. The billboards that lined the quaint streets and hairpin turns proudly proclaimed the hometown favorite to be Francesco Bernoulli. His face was everywhere.

Brent Mustangburger and Darrell Cartrip were on hand to broadcast the color and excitement. "Welcome, everyone, to the beautiful town of Porto Corsa!" Brent said into his microphone. "The big news here continues to be Allinol. Sir Miles Axlerod spoke to the media earlier today to answer questions about its safety."

Brent cut to a video of Axlerod, who seemed very distressed. "An independent panel of scientists has determined that Allinol is completely safe. Okay? Safe!" he emphatically told the reporters.

"So the race will go on," Darrell Cartrip said. "But the question everyone is asking is: Will the real Lightning McQueen show up today?"

Darrell highlighted a graphic image of the race standings, showing Francesco at the top with ten points. "Well, he'd better," Darrell said. "Talk about a hometown advantage. Francesco Bernoulli grew up racing this course!"

The announcer barely had time to introduce Francesco before the crowd began wildly chanting Francesco's name.

"Bellissima!" Francesco said, loving the adoring crowd. "Thank you for your support, and thanks to Lightning McQueen for his big mistake!"

The track announcer continued. "In the second position: *Numero Novantacinque,* Number Ninety-Five, Lightning McQueen."

The crowd cheered, but Lightning didn't seem to notice. His crew was watching him on the pit monitor.

Luigi became anxious. "Is everything okay?"

"If you're worried about your fuel, man, don't be," Fillmore said into the radio. "It's perfectly safe."

"No, guys. I just wish Mater were here," Lightning answered as he rolled into the starting grid.

The day of the big race was also the day of the meeting of the Lemonheads, the leaders of the Lemon families, in Porto Corsa. Outside the town's elegant casino, a group of rough-looking Hugos were impatiently waiting for the Lemonheads to arrive.

Ivan, the Eastern European tow truck, was telling his Hugo buddy Alexander how ugly Gremlins were, when a very pretty little sports car pulled up.

"My grandfather has broken down," Holley said

to Ivan and Alexander. "If one of you could help, I'd be so grateful." She was disguised as an Italian model, and they both fell for it.

Ivan revved his engine. "Sounds like you need some 'roadside assistance'?"

Holley nodded, and after a brief challenge from Alexander Hugo, Ivan happily followed Holley down the street.

Mater peeked around the corner and saw them coming. Suddenly, the whole plan made him nervous.

"I don't know about this," he said to Finn, who was sitting casually in an outdoor restaurant. "What if I screw things up?"

Finn smiled. "Impossible," he radioed to Mater. "Just apply the same level of dedication you've been using to play the idiot tow truck and you'll be fine."

Mater was stunned. "Wait, did you say 'idiot'? Is that how you see me?"

Finn radioed back, "Of course—that's how everyone sees you. Isn't that the idea? I tell you, that's the genius of it!" he exclaimed. "No one realizes they're being fooled because they're too busy laughing at the fool. It's brilliant!"

Suddenly, Holley turned the corned and zapped

Ivan the tow truck into unconsciousness with her electrified stun gun. She looked at Mater.

"Why aren't you in disguise?" she asked him. "Come on! There's no time."

Mater quickly deployed Holley's cloaking image to turn himself into Ivan's double and rolled toward the casino. Victor, the Lemonhead of the Hugo family, was just arriving.

"Ivan!" Victor called out. "Why do you disrespect me so by making me wait here?"

Mater quickly attached his hook to Victor's polished fender and rolled the distinguished Hugo Lemon through the casino entrance.

"He's in," Finn radioed to Holley.

16

As Mater moved through the elegant, high-ceilinged casino, he was overwhelmed by the palatial gaming room. "Wow," he said. "This place looks like it's made of gold!"

The Hugos on either side of Mater gave him funny looks. Their friend Ivan had seen this place before.

"That's because it is!" Holley said to Mater over his radio. "Be careful what you say."

"Why's that?" Mater spoke into his headset. He kept forgetting that everyone around him was listening, too!

Alexander Hugo stared at Mater. "You're acting strange today, Ivan."

Holley had also equipped Mater with a digital device to identify the cars he met. It quickly produced a readout that only Mater could see.

"Alexander Hugo, aka Chop Shop." Mater began reading out loud. "Hey, you got a lot of *aka's*, Alex. But I guess that tracks, seeing as how you're wanted in France, Germany, and the Czech Republic."

"*Mater!*" Holley screamed as her face appeared on Mater's monitor. "*Stop it!*" She knew Mater was about to blow his cover. She simply could not figure out why the American agent behaved so outrageously sometimes.

Alexander looked over at Mater.

"Keep your voice down. You're gonna get me arrested," he whispered. Then Alexander said to the other Hugos, "Don't mess with Ivan today. He's testy."

Finn and Holley stared at each other in disbelief.

"Ohhh, that was a close one," Finn commented.

Mater towed Victor into a private room. The Lemons were already seated around a large table. Holley's monitor scanned the room. Immediately, her computer began scrolling information on the Lemons.

"Maybe now we can find out who's behind all this," she said, then settled in to listen as the Lemons began a heated discussion. They seemed to be waiting to meet their mysterious leader.

Inside, Mater continued to observe.

"Is the Big Boss here yet?" Victor asked.

"No, not yet," a Trunkov replied impatiently.

WHAM! A door swung open. The room went silent as the Lemons stared at the door and waited.

And suddenly . . . Professor Z appeared!

Everyone looked disappointed. All the Lemons knew Professor Z. They wanted to meet his boss, the Big Boss, who was their true leader.

"When is he coming?" Victor, the Hugo Lemonhead, demanded.

Professor Z smiled slyly.

"He's already here," he announced.

A bank of monitors that lined the back wall suddenly crackled to life. An image appeared. It was an image of an engine.

Mater stifled a gasp. He recognized it as the engine that belonged to the car that was leading the whole operation. It was that Lemon engine with the Whitworth bolts!

It was a live feed. The voice of the Big Boss was electronically distorted so that he couldn't be identified. Everyone in the room stared at his engine—a bad Lemon engine that was being repaired—as its owner spoke to the Lemons.

"Welcome, everyone," the voice announced over the video feed. "I wish I could be with you on this very special day. But with my clutch assembly broken, you know how it is."

The Lemons all nodded. Every single Lemon knew what it was like to live a life disrupted by constant repairs. They had wanted to see the Big Boss, but they understood his situation.

Outside, Finn desperately asked Holley to unscramble the voice of this mysterious leader. They had to find out his identity!

"Trying," Holley muttered as she worked. "I can't. It's too sophisticated."

Inside the casino, the disguised voice of the mysterious, evil leader continued: "We're here to celebrate. Today, all of your hard work pays off. The world turned their backs on cars like us. They stopped manufacturing us, stopped making our parts. The only thing they haven't stopped doing is laughing at us!"

The mastermind behind this terrible plot continued to rally his fellow Lemons: "They've called us terrible names: jalopy, rust bucket, heap, clunker, junker . . . *Lemon!*"

The cars grumbled in agreement.

The voice continued, "But what they consider taunts just give us strength, because today, my friends, that all ends."

BOOM! Mater jumped as the video monitors showed the racer Carla Velosa on the course with smoke pouring from her engine.

"They laughed at us!" the distorted voice continued. "Now it's our turn to laugh back! They called us Lemon! Embrace it!"

BOOM! Another racer's engine blew up.

Outside, Finn and Holley were desperately trying to figure out what was going on.

"I'm detecting high levels of electromagnetic radiation!" Holley reported. Working swiftly, she traced it until she zeroed in on the point of origin. Focusing with her binoculars, she saw Grem and Acer with the fake WGP camera aimed at the racecourse.

"Finn! It's the camera!" she cried.

"Where?" Finn shouted.

"On the tower!"

Finn took off at top speed, racing along the winding cliff roads toward the WGP camera. He needed to stop Grem and Acer fast, before more racers were injured.

Mater continued to listen to the mysterious car who

was the mastermind behind this explosive operation.

"This was to be alternative fuel's moment in the sun. But after today, everyone will race back to gasoline. And we, the owners of the largest untapped oil reserve in the world, will become the most powerful cars in the world! They will need us. And they will finally respect us!"

Mater gasped as the roomful of Lemons burst out into cheers.

17

Finn zigzagged up the steep cliff until he reached a large crevasse. He could see Grem and Acer on the opposite side, holding the WGP camera. Finn hit the gas and leaped toward the two Lemons.

That was when Finn felt himself freeze in midair. A helicopter had captured him with a large magnet.

Grem and Acer started laughing at Finn.

"We figured you might stop by," Acer shouted to Finn. The two Lemons gleefully turned back to the camera and aimed it at Number 4, Max Schnell. This time it was Grem's turn to zap the racer.

Down on the racecourse, plumes of smoke suddenly billowed from Number 4. The car swerved out of control and crashed into another racer, sending them both tumbling. The crowd gasped when another car—Shu Todoroki—spun out as his engine exploded in black smoke. Grem and Acer chuckled as they watched the car skid to the railing, taking two others with it. The race was becoming a monster pileup.

Up ahead at the finish line, Lightning and Francesco were still battling it out for the win. They had no idea what was happening on the track behind them. Each was focused on winning!

"*Ka-chow!*" Lightning shouted as he narrowly crossed the finish line first. He was about to thoroughly enjoy beating Francesco when he saw the smoke rising from the multiple car wreck.

"Oh, no," Lightning said to himself.

It wasn't long before Sir Miles Axlerod had to face the media. The reporters all demanded to know whether the last race, in London, would be run on Allinol. Was it causing the race cars to crash?

Axlerod seemed completely defeated.

"I cannot in good conscience risk the lives of any more race cars," he told the anxious reporters. "The final race will not be run on Allinol."

Inside the casino, the Lemons were still cheering when Lightning suddenly appeared on the screen.

The room went quiet as Lightning announced that he would still use Allinol in the last race.

"My friend Fillmore says the fuel's safe," he told reporters. "And that's good enough for me."

Mater held his breath as he watched Lightning add: "I didn't stand by a friend of mine recently. I'm not making the same mistake twice."

The sound of a ringing phone suddenly cut through the silent casino. Professor Z quickly answered it. It was the Big Boss.

"Yes, sir. Of course," he said into the phone.

He turned to the Lemons and announced what the Big Boss had said: "Allinol must be finished for good. Lightning McQueen cannot win the last race." The Lemons *had* to stop Lightning.

Mater's eyes grew wide. Professor Z was going to ask Grem and Acer to take aim at Lightning next!

"No!" Mater said. He turned to leave and banged his hood on a chandelier. An electric jolt passed through him—just enough to cause his holographic disguise to disappear. The Lemons stared in shock as Mater turned into his rusty old tow truck self.

"The American spy!" Professor Z said. The Lemons immediately drew their weapons.

"Dadgum!" Mater said into his radio.

"Gaitlin gun. Request acknowledged," Mater's computer answered.

Mater was shocked to see guns roll out of both of his side doors.

"Shoot. I didn't mean—" Mater tried to say as he suddenly sprayed the ceiling with bullets.

Mater was thrown back by the force of one of his guns. "Whoa! Wait!" he hollered. "I didn't mean *that* kind of shoot!"

"Correction acknowledged," the computer replied. "Deploying parachute."

With a whoosh, a large parachute shot out from Mater's undercarriage. In seconds, he was dragged out onto the casino's balcony.

"Whoa!" Mater cried as the chute filled with air and hoisted him into the sky.

Mater drifted over the town of Porto Corsa until he spotted a motorboat speeding through the water below. He dropped his tow hook and hitched a ride toward the race site. There was no time to lose. He had to get to Lightning and warn him.

Mater could see Lightning onstage, talking to the reporters, as he dropped into the crowd.

"Lemme through!" Mater shouted as he tried to make his way to the stage.

"Back up, sir," a security guard told Mater, who was frantic with worry.

Mater kept pushing through the crowd.

"We have a lunatic at gate nine," the guard said into his walkie-talkie.

"No, listen!" Mater sputtered. "I—I was disguised as a tow truck with some Lemons, and they got this ray-gun plot!"

"Repeat. Lunatic at gate nine," the guard said.

Mater could still see Lightning onstage. He used all his tow truck weight to keep pushing through the throngs of cars. "Comin' through. Life-or-death situation here," he said as he tried to move forward. But no one seemed to believe him.

18

As additional security closed in on Mater, he yelled, "Lightning McQueen, if you're out there, *they're gonna kill you!*"

Lightning suddenly looked up. He saw a tow hook moving through the crowd.

"Mater!" he called out. Lightning drove off the stage and pushed through the throng. He kept tracking the tow hook, only to find it wasn't Mater at all. It was the Lemon driver, Ivan.

"Sorry," Lightning said, filled with confusion and disappointment. He could have sworn he had heard his buddy Mater.

As Lightning was led back to the stage, Ivan breathed a sigh of relief. He had done his job by distracting Lightning while Professor Z's Lemons hijacked Mater! Now Mater was in the back of a transport vehicle. Nobody objected to seeing the lunatic tow truck being hauled away.

"Let me go!" Mater yelled. Professor Z just smiled.

"You really care about that race car. Fascinating," he said as he slammed the doors of the transport. Professor Z released a sleeping gas into the small space where Mater was trapped. "Pity you didn't warn him about it in time."

Mater's eyes slowly closed, and he tipped over like a fallen tree. He dreamed about everything that had happened over the past days: how Finn had called him an idiot, how he had called in to *The Mel Dorado Show* and said that Lightning was the fastest car in the world, how he had embarrassed Lightning at the WGP racers' party—and how he had caused Lightning to lose the first race of the World Grand Prix. Maybe Mater *was* an idiot, just as Finn had said.

Bong! Bong! Bong!

Mater's eyes suddenly snapped open. He was awake but couldn't get his bearings. He was hanging upside down, and his whole body was aching. Now all he could hear was a very loud *click-click-click*.

Mater looked around and saw nothing but enormous, churning gears. And then he figured it out: he was inside the workings of a huge clock. He spotted Finn and Holley strapped bumper to bumper nearby. Professor Z and the Lemons had caught all three of them.

"Holley! Finn!" Mater cried out. "Where are we?"

"We're in London, Mater."

Mater had heard of a famous old clock in London. Now he was trapped inside it. As the clock's gears— and the cars' life spans—ticked away, Mater told Finn and Holley, "This is all my fault."

"Don't be a fool," Finn replied.

"But I am," Mater said. "Remember? You said so."

"No," Finn said, then tried to explain. "I was complimenting you on what a good spy you were."

"But I'm not a spy," Mater said. "Been trying to tell you that this whole time. I'm just a rusty tow truck."

Holley realized that Mater was telling the truth. "Finn, he's not joking," she said.

But Finn didn't need to be told. "I know," he replied. He had finally realized that Mater was no secret agent. He really was just a regular truck.

"You were right, Finn," Mater said sadly. "I'm just a fool. And what's happened to Lightning is all my fault."

Finn was about to object when the doors of the clock tower opened. Grem and Acer rolled in. They pulled a sheet away from a window. The WGP camera was set up and aimed toward the streets of London.

"Professor Z wanted you to have a front-row seat for the death of Lightning McQueen," Grem said to Mater.

"He's still alive?" Mater asked hopefully.

"Not for much longer," Acer replied as he focused the camera on the street below—a street that was part of the racecourse where Lightning McQueen would soon be driving.

Down in Lightning McQueen's pit, the whole Radiator Springs gang was gathered. They had all traveled to London. Sally, Flo, Ramone, and Sarge were there. Even Red, the town's fire truck, had shown up. They had all come for the same reason: to find and help their friend Mater. All they knew was that he had never made it home to Radiator Springs.

"Sarge is in touch with the British military," Ramone told Lightning, hoping it would ease his mind. Lightning was seriously worried about his best friend, especially after thinking he had seen him at the track—and then lost him. Little did Lightning know that his own life was in danger, and that Mater was equally worried about him!

"You just need to focus," Sally told Lightning. But he couldn't bring himself to do it.

He was about to drop out of the race when Sir Miles Axlerod approached the pit.

"I just wanted to come down here and thank you," Sir Miles said to Lightning. "After Italy, I was finished. And then you gave me one last shot. And I probably shouldn't be saying this at all, but I hope you win today. You show the world that they've been wrong about Allinol."

Lightning looked at his friends. He couldn't drop out of the race now.

"It's what Mater would have wanted," Sally said to Lightning.

It was true. Mater would want him to race. Moments later, a very determined Lightning zoomed to the starting line. It was the only thing he could think to do for Mater. The race was on!

From up in the clock tower, Grem grinned as he heard the roar of engines.

The race had begun, and the cars in the lead were getting closer and closer to the giant clock. Soon they would race right by Professor Z's two thugs and their deadly "camera."

"Here they come!" Grem suddenly shouted. He turned up the juice on the WGP camera—to its highest level—and aimed it at Lightning.

19

Mater closed his eyes. He couldn't stand to see his friend hurt. Finn and Holley were helpless, too. They saw Grem pull the trigger.

But Lightning zoomed right past the clock tower unharmed. He hadn't even slowed down!

Grem and Acer were shocked. Professor Z radioed them immediately.

"What happened?" the Professor demanded.

"You broke it," Acer said to Grem.

Grem listened to Professor Z on the radio. "I understand," Grem said. "Yes, sir."

"What'd he say?" Acer asked anxiously.

"We go to the backup plan," Grem said, and they both headed for the doors.

"Backup plan?" Mater called to them.

Grem gave Mater a nasty laugh and said, "Yeah,

we snuck a bomb into Lightning McQueen's pit."

"The next time he makes a stop, instead of saying 'Ka-chow,' he's gonna go *ka-boom!*" Acer added.

"Dadgum Lemons," Mater muttered out of a mix of anger and frustration. Of course, his computer heard "gum" and spun out his weaponry.

The Lemons left the tower, laughing. But Mater noticed that the spinning barrels of his weapons had begun to shave away at the restraints that tied him to the clock's gears!

"Dadgum! Dadgum! Dadgum!" Mater shouted excitedly. It worked! The guns spun away at the restraints until they broke. Mater suddenly dropped toward the whirring gears of the clock.

He quickly whipped out his tow cable and hooked it onto a pipe. He swung himself toward the doors and landed with a thud.

"I gotta get y'all out of there so you can save Lightning McQueen," he said, looking up at Finn and Holley in desperation.

"There's no time!" Finn told him. "It's up to you now. We'll be okay."

Holley said, "Go get some more dents, Mater!" Mater gave Holley a smile and shot out of the door.

"So, we're going to be okay?" Holley asked Finn.

Finn shrugged. "He wouldn't have left if I'd told him the truth." They both watched as a giant gear moved one click closer to crushing them completely. "Being killed by a clock: gives a whole new meaning to 'Your time has come.'"

That gave Holley an idea. She fired at the clock's gearbox, sending a blast of electricity through the wires and into the gears.

"What are you doing?" Finn asked as a shower of sparks flew through the clock tower.

"Trying to turn back time," she answered. "If I can reverse the polarity . . ." She strained to get off another shot. This time, she scored a direct hit. The clock stopped with a jolt and then reversed itself. The gears began to move away from them.

"Quick thinking, Holley!" Finn said, impressed.

But a different gear was now moving closer—a gear that was going to smash in their trunks.

"Drive, Holley!" Finn said as the gear began to move over them.

Chrome was ground off their rear bumpers as the two spun their wheels. They inched just far enough apart to evade the giant machinery—but not too far. The gear sliced right through the cable that had them tied bumper to bumper! Finn and Holley flew to opposite platforms inside the clock.

They were free!

"We've got to get to the course!" Finn shouted. "Calculate the fastest way to get there!"

Holley instantly popped out two wings from her side panels. She could see the shock on Finn's face.

"They're standard issue now," she told him.

"You kids get all the good hardware," he said with a smile. He was impressed with Agent Shiftwell. As they headed out the door, Holley noticed an air filter on the ground.

"Isn't that Mater's?" she asked.

They looked at each other and realized that one of Mater's parts had been taken out and replaced. It could mean only one thing: Professor Z had planted the bomb inside Mater!

"I knew his escape was too easy," Finn muttered.

20

Meanwhile, Mater zoomed through London. He had to get to Lightning and warn him about the bomb in his pit. When Mater finally got to the track, he drove through all the pits until he got to Lightning's.

"Mater!" Luigi cried out in surprise.

"Everybody, get out! Y'all gotta get out of the pits now!" Mater shouted. He looked around and saw the entire Radiator Springs gang in the pit.

"Wh-what are you guys doing here?" he sputtered.

"We're all here because of you," Sally told him. "Is everything okay?"

"No! Everything is not okay! There's a bomb in here! You guys gotta get out now!"

Suddenly, Mater heard Finn over his radio. Finn was driving through the streets of London as Holley flew above him.

"Mater, listen to me," Finn said. "The bomb is on you! They knew you'd try to help Lightning McQueen, so they planted it in your air filter when you were knocked out."

Mater was shocked. He snorted and blew his air filter cover off. It was true! Mater could see the bomb attached to his engine. Then he looked up and saw Lightning, grinning and racing right toward him.

"Mater!" Lightning called out from the track where he was racing neck and neck with the other cars. "I've been so worried about you!"

Up in the stands, Professor Z was watching from his private box. He was waiting for Lightning to get close enough to Mater. Then he would press the detonator and get rid of them both!

Just as Lightning was about to enter the pit, Mater cried out, "Stay away from me!" Wildly, Mater spun out and started driving backward onto the track.

"That's not going to happen this time," Lightning said, and drove faster, trying to catch up with Mater. "I'm sticking by you the way you always stick by me! I just want a chance to explain myself. Please stop!"

Lightning sped up even more. "I'm not letting you get away again!" he said as he zoomed within inches of Mater's bumper, desperately trying to latch on to Mater's hook. Professor Z smiled and rolled his front tire toward the detonator.

In a panic, Mater shouted to his computer, "Gotta get away from Lightning!"

Mater's secret-agent computer answered: "Request acknowledged."

Professor Z was just about to press the detonator when a rocket in Mater's arsenal blasted him forward. Professor Z was furious when his detonator flashed TARGET OUT OF RANGE.

Lightning, stunned, continued to chase Mater. He had never seen his buddy race at such a high speed. Mater whizzed past Francesco and crashed through a fence. Mater was causing chaos right in the middle of the World Grand Prix racing course!

Lightning took the opportunity to catch up with his buddy. This time, he latched on to Mater's hook and held on tight.

In Lightning McQueen's pit, the Radiator Springs gang watched their television monitor in shock. They heard Brent Mustangburger say, "And Lightning McQueen just blasted away, hooked to a rocket-propelled tow truck."

From his private box, Professor Z was still pressing the detonator, hoping something would happen. He suddenly saw Holley appear in front of his window. She was hovering in midair. Professor Z quickly realized that her presence could mean nothing but trouble for him. He panicked and raced away, leaving the detonator behind.

Hovering near Professor Z, the Lemons howled, "Get Lightning McQueen!" They remembered Professor Z's warning that there would be no Lemon victory unless Allinol and Lightning McQueen were both ruined.

On the streets of London, Professor Z was beating a hasty retreat when Finn McMissile caught a glimpse of him zooming down a side street. In a flash, the secret agent was on the Professor's tail, desperately trying to capture him.

Finn urgently radioed Holley with a plan: "I'll get Professor Z! You help Mater!"

Holley, who was still in the air, radiocd, "Got it!" She quickly flew over Francesco, turned a corner, and disappeared from sight.

"What is happening?" Francesco asked. Everything seemed to be faster than Francesco today.

Finn screamed around a corner, only to see Professor Z speeding toward a large combat ship. The ship was casting off its lines, ready to set sail. Professor Z had signaled ahead for the ship to be ready for his escape.

"Hurry, Professor!" the combat ship said.

Professor Z suddenly felt himself jolt backward. Finn had tethered him by deploying tensile cables to his rear bumper.

Finn began reeling him in. "Did you really think I'd let you just float away, Professor Z?"

But Finn was wrong. He had more than Professor Z to fight. An ultrapowerful electromagnet on the combat ship rapidly pulled both cars toward it.

"Give it up, McMissile," Professor Z said smugly.

But Finn McMissile was not one to give up easily. He let loose every weapon in his arsenal. The weapons were all instantly sucked up onto the magnet.

KA-BOOOOM!

Flames from the exploding combat ship could be seen from miles away. There was no time to lose. Finn sped off to find Holley and Mater.

At that same moment, Mater was back down on the street with Lightning in tow. Holley was flying high above, trying to watch over them, when she heard the explosion. She tried to put it out of her mind, hoping that Finn was okay. She knew that, no matter what, Finn would want her to save Mater and get rid of that bomb.

From her bird's-eye view, Holley could see Grem and Acer just one block away from Mater. The two Lemons were about to cross an intersection and hit the tow truck broadside.

"Oh, no," Holley said to herself.

21

Agent Shiftwell swiftly dropped to the street and deliberately skidded into Grem and Acer's path. She was putting herself at risk to save Mater. Unable to stop, the two Lemons flipped over Holley and landed in a waste-disposal truck. Agent Holley Shiftwell had just received her first dent—and she had gotten it by helping out a friend.

Quickly she turned to that friend, Mater, and electronically scanned his air filter. "We've got to get that bomb off you!"

"Bomb?" Lightning repeated, finally noticing the bomb attached to Mater.

"Yeah, they strapped it to me," Mater explained. It was the Lemons' backup plan to stop Lightning.

Lightning suddenly understood why Mater had been trying to get away from him.

"Mater," he said, "who put a bomb on you?"

Just then Professor Z rolled up. He was completely entangled in Finn's cables and tensile lines. Finn was holding on to him as if the Professor were on a leash.

"You!" Professor Z moaned when he saw Lightning.

Finn cut the conversation short. "Turn off the bomb, Professor Z!"

But Professor Z simply smirked. "Are you all so dimwitted? It's voice-activated. Everything's voice-activated these days."

Mater had gotten a little used to this voice-activated stuff. He jumped right in and said, "Deactivate! Deactivate!"

Professor Z laughed as he saw everyone's expressions turn to looks of horror. Mater's voice had activated a timer on the bomb. They had four minutes—and counting—before it would explode.

"Did I forget to mention it can only be disarmed by the one who activated it?" Professor Z asked.

Holley charged up to the Professor's grille. "Say it!" she ordered him.

"Deactivate," Professor Z said calmly. The bomb suddenly lost a minute. It was now going to explode in less than three minutes! Professor Z grinned as the seconds ticked away. "I am not the one who activated it. Would anyone else like to try?"

Holley turned to Professor Z and hit him with a jolt from her electrified stun gun.

Finn was growing to appreciate Holley's instincts more and more. "You read my mind," he said to her as Professor Z fell over.

But the bomb was still ticking.

"What do we do?" Lightning asked.

"You blow up," Victor replied simply. The head of the Hugo Lemon family had rolled next to the Professor. His Lemon relatives were blocking the entrance to the side street.

The other Lemons and their families blocked all the other streets. The Lemons revved their feeble engines, ready to charge.

Lightning took one look at Mater and sighed. "I'm gonna go out on a limb here. These are the guys that want me dead?"

Mater faced the Lemons. "Fellas, listen," he begged. "I know what you're going through. Cars have been laughing at me my whole life, too. But is hurting folks and making money really gonna make you feel better?"

The Lemons stopped. They looked at one another.

Then one of the Lemons in front shrugged and said, "It's worth a shot."

A gang of Hugos, Pacers, Zapors, and Gremlins rushed toward Lightning. The Gremlin Lemon was leading the charge when he was suddenly broadsided by a blast of water.

It was Red, the fire truck, spraying his powerful fire hose! And the rest of the Radiator Springs gang was with him. Even Flo was ready to rumble. They drove at the Lemons full-force.

Guido zipped off some Lemon tires with his air gun as Flo blinded them with her high beams. In seconds, Guido had another stack of lug nuts next to him.

Ramone spray-painted their windshields so the Lemons couldn't see. Finn, who'd lost all his weapons to the combat ship's magnet, used his karate skills to take out Lemons three and four at a time. Soon the streets were littered with cheap cars.

"Retreat!" a Gremlin hollered.

As the few remaining Lemons scattered, Guido rushed to Mater's side. He tried every wrench in his tool case, but not a single one of them could take the bolts off the bomb.

Cross-eyed, Mater took a good look at the bolts. Then it all became clear.

"I get it! I get it!" he cried. "I know what needs to be done!"

"Then do it!" Lightning urged his friend.

"No! I can't!" Mater answered. Then he whispered to Lightning: "Nobody takes me seriously. I know that now. This ain't Radiator Springs."

"Yes, it is," Lightning replied firmly. He continued, "You're yourself in Radiator Springs. Be yourself here! If folks aren't taking you seriously, then *they* need to change. Not you! I know that, because I didn't take you seriously before, and I was wrong. Now, you can do this! You're the bomb!"

Mater beamed. "Thanks, buddy."

"No, you're the *actual bomb*! Now let's go!" Lightning shouted.

Mater latched his hook on to Lightning, and they took off at top speed.

22

"**C**omputer," Mater said, zooming down a side street. "I need the thing you did before to get me away from Lightning."

"Request acknowledged," the computer responded. Lightning was more than a little surprised to hear Mater talking to a computer. He was even more surprised when the rocket thrusters kicked in.

Lightning and Mater, still hooked together, were catapulted toward a wall. Mater screamed to the computer, "Now I need you to do the chute—the second kind, not the first!"

"*Ahhhh!*" Lightning yelled. He closed his eyes and heard a swooshing sound. Then he felt air beneath his tires. Lightning didn't understand, but Mater's chute had popped open. The two best friends from Radiator Springs were airborne over London!

Mater steered the chute toward Buckingham Palace. The Queen of England stood on a balcony, surrounded by an audience of dignitaries, including Sir Miles Axlerod. They were gathering to celebrate the completion of the World Grand Prix.

"Who's winning the race?" the Queen was asking one of her attendants, when Mater and Lightning suddenly dropped from the sky.

"Look out below!" Mater shouted.

"Back up! Back up!" the royal guards yelled. "Stand back!"

The Queen smiled. "Lightning McQueen!" she said brightly, recognizing the international racer.

"It's okay!" Lightning tried to tell the crowd. "Mater has something to say. Go, Mater!"

Mater felt everyone's gaze turn to him. "Okay!" he said, trying to gather his thoughts. "Someone's been sabotaging the racers and hurting the cars, and I know who! Oh, wait! Your Majesty!"

Mater realized he had forgotten to bow. As he leaned over, everyone saw the ticking time bomb!

"He's got a bomb!" the guards yelled, jumping into action. "Get down now!"

"Hold your fire!" It was Finn McMissile. The agent

had tracked Mater to the palace, along with Agent Shiftwell. "You could hit the bomb!"

Finn and Holley raced toward Mater. Finn dove and rolled quickly to place himself between Mater and the Queen. He trusted Mater, but he had to protect the Queen!

"Mater," Finn said calmly, "I don't know what you're doing, but stand down now!"

Lightning nudged his friend. "Mater, just cut to the chase!"

"Okay!" Mater cried. Then he turned toward Sir Miles Axlerod. "It's him."

"What?" Axlerod exclaimed. "Me? You've got to be crazy!"

Mater continued: "I figured it out when I realized y'all attached this ticking time bomb with Whitworth bolts—the same bolts that hold together this crummy old engine from the photograph. And then I remembered what they say about old British engines: If there ain't no oil under them, there ain't no oil in them."

Axlerod was beside himself. The bomb was ticking. *"What is he talking about?"* he exclaimed.

Mater looked Sir Miles Axlerod straight in the

eyes. "It was you leaking oil at the party in Japan. You just blamed it on me."

"Electric cars don't use oil, you—you twit!" Axlerod stammered.

"Then you're faking it!" Mater shouted, filled with confidence. "You didn't convert to no electric. We pop that hood, and we're gonna see that Lemon engine from that picture right there."

But as Mater moved toward Axlerod to pop his hood, Holley spoke up. "Axlerod created the race, Mater. Why would he want to hurt anyone?"

"To make Allinol look bad, so everyone would go back to oil," Mater replied firmly. "He said it himself with his disguised voice in that casino."

"Mater," Finn said. "He created Allinol."

"Yeah," Mater said, "but what if he found that huge oil field just as the world was trying to find something else? What if he came up with Allinol just to make alternative fuel look bad?"

Now Mater had the attention of Holley and Finn. They all moved in toward Axlerod.

"Keep away, you idiot!" Axlerod screamed at Mater. There were exactly eight seconds left before the bomb would explode! "You're insane! You are!"

And then Axlerod said it: "Deactivate!"

The bomb stopped ticking.

"Bomb deactivated," a computer voice announced. "Have a nice day, Sir Miles." That proved it. Axlerod was the only voice that could deactivate the bomb. He was the Lemon behind the plot.

The following day at Buckingham Palace, Mater was knighted by the Queen. The rusty tow truck bowed deeply as the Queen said, "I dub thee Sir Mater."

Mater looked up. "Sir?" he asked the Queen. "Why, you can call me Mater, Your Majesty. I don't want to hear none of this 'Sir' business. By the way, have y'all met each other? Queen? Lightning McQueen. Lightning McQueen, Queen. Queen? McMissile. McMissile, Queen." Mater went on with his introductions as the crowds cheered their new hero—the hero who had shown the courage and intelligence needed to save them and the rest of the world, too.

23

Back in Radiator Springs, the town put up a new sign. It read: WELCOME TO RADIATOR SPRINGS– HOME OF LIGHTNING MCQUEEN AND SIR TOW MATER.

Mobs of tourists had shown up to see the final race of the World Grand Prix. All the racers who'd never gotten to finish the race in London were there, too, including Francesco Bernoulli. But all the attention was on Mater.

"So were you really a spy?" one of the tourists asked Sir Tow Mater.

"Tell us everything!" another said.

Mater told them about taking a spy jet to Paris.

"Did that really happen?" a car in the crowd asked. "A spy jet? Come on."

Just then they heard Siddeley, the spy jet, overhead.

Siddeley made a perfectly smooth landing right next to the Cozy Cone Motel at the edge of town.

"You're right. It does sound a little farfetched," the sleek jet joked dryly.

"Sid!" Mater shouted. He saw Finn and Holley exit the plane. "What are y'all doing here?"

"We hear that there's a special competition here today," Holley said.

Luigi rolled up. "So you got my email!" he said as the whole Radiator Springs gang gathered around.

Mater suddenly noticed the dent in Holley's side. It was the dent she'd gotten when she saved Mater from Grem and Acer. Mater hadn't noticed it earlier.

"Don't worry," Mater said gently. "My buddy Ramone can fix that dent for you in no time."

Holley smiled. "Oh, no, I'm keeping that dent," she said. "It's way too valuable."

"A valuable dent?" Luigi said to Guido. "She's as crazy as Mater."

Holley and Mater shared a laugh. Maybe spies could have friends after all.

Lightning rolled up and asked why his engine hadn't exploded when the WGP camera beam hit it.

"We couldn't figure that one out, either," Finn

said as he looked around at Mater's hometown.

"Our investigation proved that Allinol was a fake," Holley explained. "It wasn't really an alternative fuel at all. And Axlerod engineered it so that when it got hit by the beam, it would explode."

Lightning turned to Fillmore. "Wait a second. Fillmore, you said my fuel was safe."

Everyone turned to Fillmore. "If you're implying I switched out that rotgut excuse for alternative fuel with my all-natural, organic biofuel just because I never trusted Axlerod, you're dead wrong. It was him," Fillmore announced. He was looking right at Sarge.

Sarge just shrugged. "Once 'big oil,' always 'big oil' . . . man."

"Tree hugger," Fillmore fired back.

Sheriff's voice suddenly came over the loudspeaker. "The Radiator Springs Grand Prix is about to start!"

As the racers moved to the starting line, Francesco caught up with Lightning and Sally.

"Francesco!" Lightning greeted him. "I'd like you to meet Sally."

"Signorina Sally," Francesco said, and bowed, enoying the introduction. "It is official. Lightning McQueen is the luckiest car in the world—which he will have to be to have a chance against Francesco today."

Francesco noticed a sticker on Lightning's rear bumper and asked, "What is that?"

Francesco got closer. "'Ka-*ciao*, Francesco,'" he said, reading the bumper sticker. "I get it. *Ciao. Ka-ciao*. Is your cute little thing you say. Very clever. Not as clever as Francesco when he say it first."

As Lightning and Sally turned to leave, Sally said, "Okay, so he's not that great."

Lightning just smiled.

As the racers pulled into position, Finn and Holley were getting ready to leave. They heard the sound of engines zooming through the desert as they headed toward their jet.

"You're leaving already?" Mater asked them.

"We've got another mission," Finn told him. "Just stopped by to pick something up on the way."

Holley and Finn were now partners. They wanted Mater to join them.

"Her Majesty asked for you personally, Mater," Finn said, holding out one last hope.

Mater grinned. He wasn't a stupid tow truck after all. He was so dang smart that they wanted him to work with them as a bona fide, honest-to-goodness secret agent.

"Well, thanks," he said, meaning it. "But as much fun as it was with y'all, this is where I belong." He was glad everyone thought he was smart, but he was even happier to be with his friends.

"We understand," Finn replied. "Although if there's ever anything I can do for you, just let me know."

Mater paused, but not for more than a second. "Actually, there is one thing," he said, grinning.

Moments later, Mater was zooming past every race car on the course. *"Woo-hoo!"* he hollered when he caught up to Lightning.

"Mater?" Lightning shouted in surprise.

"Check it out!" Mater yelled back, grinning. "They let me keep the rockets!"

The two hometown favorites—and best buddies—laughed out loud as they raced side by side toward the finish line.